CLARISSA WILD

Copyright © 2022 Clarissa Wild
All rights reserved.
ISBN: 9798844555626

This is a work of fiction. Names, characters, places and incidents are either the product of the author's imagination or are used fictitiously. Any resemblance to actual events, places, organizations, or person, whether living or dead, is entirely coincidental.

All rights reserved. No part of this book may be reproduced, transmitted in any form or by any means, electronic or mechanical, including photocopying, recording, or by any information storage retrieval system. Doing so would break licensing and copyright laws.

One

Aurora

In my purple dress, I run as hard as I can without looking back.

Into the darkness, into my biggest fear.

Complete and utter loneliness.

Even though tears run freely across my cheeks and my legs quake from the adrenaline, I keep going, far beyond the doors to the warehouse, across the pier, and into a narrow alley. I zigzag between the buildings. Ignoring the pain in my feet and muscles, I keep going, past all the warehouses, until I finally reach a road.

Pausing, I take a huge breath while bent over with my hands on my knees.

I gaze down at the pavement and at the salty droplets that slowly begin to cover it. Each one of those specks is a scream swallowed back down.

Don't break down. Not yet.

I blow out a big breath and continue running, pushing back the sting of regret.

I have to keep going.

For him.

"Aurora."

A familiar voice suddenly makes me stop and almost tumble forward.

Looking around, I only see warehouses and giant dumpsters. To the left, behind all the alleys, is an endless sea.

"Here."

The voice comes from behind one of the dumpsters. And it's definitely a guy, but he sounds like a mess.

Should I see who's behind it? Or run like hell?

The same guy groans in pain.

How could I ignore that?

I sigh out loud but quickly make my way to the dumpsters to my right. My eyes widen the second I spot who's lying in the rubble.

"Papa," I mutter, and I rush over to him, only to stop mere inches away when our eyes connect, and I remember what he'd said to me.

I don't even want her. I never did.
She's a monster.

I swallow away the lump in my throat.

"Please …" he mutters, his breathing ragged. Uneven.

His body contains gashes and bruises from the torture Lex's men did to him. God knows what else they subjected him to. He looks completely spent.

"Help me." The visceral pain in his voice is hard to take.

He reaches for me but never comes close as his hand drops down to his body in defeat. And I blink away a couple of my tears.

I hate him for what he said.

But he's still my father.

And he's begging for help.

I push away the shame and kneel in front of him.

"Please … help me stand," he murmurs.

I sigh and nod. Then I place my arm underneath his shoulder and help him get up from the ground.

"Can you walk?" I ask.

He nods. "Barely."

"We need to get out of here. Fast," I reply.

He groans in pain but allows me to move him. Every step he takes weighs down on me, but I do my best to carry him as we walk away from the alley. It doesn't take him long to get the hang of walking in pain. Every once in a while, he hisses and clamps his teeth, his face contorting from the agony, but it does little to my frozen heart.

Still, I couldn't leave him there to die.

"Check every fucking warehouse!"

My pupils dilate, and I glare up beyond the road we're

on.

Lex's guards.

"Duck," I bark at my father, who immediately hides behind a big machine standing outside a warehouse. I help him stay put without falling over, but his sheer weight strains my muscles.

Sweat drops roll all over my face and back. There's no time to process what happened or think about any of the wounds on my body or my father's. And no time to think about Beast being left alone to die.

I gulp down my nerves as several guards run past us, oblivious to our location.

I can't let all the effort Beast did to save me go in vain.

"When they're gone, run toward the streets as fast as you can," I hiss at my father.

"Fine," he growls. "But I won't be able to walk for a long time after. Everything hurts."

"Ignore the pain until we get to safety," I say, and I peer beyond the contraption.

They seem to have rushed off in the opposite direction. I don't see them anymore, and I don't hear their voices either.

"C'mon." I push my arm underneath his shoulder again and help him up.

Helping someone this heavy walk when you're small yourself is hard, but I pull through without complaining. Though this dress isn't helping me get far quickly enough.

I drag my father across the pier and into a busy street.

We cross and head right into the main part of the city where it's bustling, even at night time. The more people around us, the safer we are. No one will try to take us out among a crowd.

"Everyone's looking at me," my father mutters, eyeing the people who glare at his wounds.

"Of course," I say. "You're bleeding."

My father glances over his shoulder. "I'm leaving a trail."

I gaze at the tiny spots of blood all over the pavement. "We just have to keep going. Somewhere."

"Where?" he asks.

I sigh. "I don't know."

I look around to try to think of a solution to our problem, but I don't know where to go.

"There," my father says, and he points at a dingy hotel at the end of the street.

"Is it safe?"

"Yes," he replies.

"But I don't have any money," I say.

"I do," he says, looking directly into my eyes.

I nod, despite my reservations. I don't know where he got the money or who got killed to get it, but right now, our options are thin.

I walk with him to the hotel, ignoring the people who stare, hoping they won't try to dissuade us from going inside or worse … contact the police.

If I know anything about my father's dealings, it's that

the police are not your friends. And I'm definitely not up for losing anyone to any kind of prison right now, no matter how much they deserve it.

"In here," my father says, pointing at a door not at the front of the building.

I frown but still do what he says, and I push open a door and move him inside. He sits down on a chair next to the door while I catch my breath for a second.

"Excuse me, can I help you?"

A man sits behind a tiny desk in front of us.

"Yeah," my father mutters. "I'm a friend."

The man narrows his eyes at us. "Blom. You're back."

He knows my father?

How often did he come here?

My father clears his throat. "I want to book a room."

"You're asking a lot right now."

My father gets up from the chair, and I help him walk toward the desk. He fishes a wad of cash from his pocket and throws it under the man's nose. The euro bills are covered in blood.

"I'll offer you double this time."

The man picks up the money, carefully checking it before counting it. Then he gazes up at us. "Fine. But only for two days. And I need you to provide a—"

My father smashes down a passport with a name on it that I don't recognize. But it's his picture.

"This good?" he asks.

Why does this feel like some back-alley deal?

The man nods, eyeing me down now. "And her?"

"No one will come looking for her," he says, but then my father puts down some extra cash. "For the trouble."

The man licks his thin lips and packs the money before shoving it in some type of register underneath the desk. Then he places a key on top and slides it our way. "Door is to the left. Two staircases and two more doors will get you to the main hotel via a side entrance. No need to check in. Just go to the room that's on your key. Don't use the elevators, and don't talk to anyone. Do not mention your names."

Jesus. What kind of hotel is this?

Not the legal kind, that's for sure. But I guess it's better than staying out in the streets.

My father takes the key, and we turn around and head for the door he mentioned.

"Oh, and don't drip blood on the carpet, please." When I glance over my shoulder at the man, he adds a creepy smile. "It just got cleaned."

My father simply throws his hand up in the air as we walk through the door.

"What is this place?" I mutter as I gaze up the two flights of stairs.

"A stairwell," my father replies.

"No, I mean this hotel thing," I say. "It's not exactly legal, is it?"

"No," my father replies. "But this hotel caters to anyone who brings money, and that's all that matters."

"So mobsters stay here?" I gulp. "Mobsters like—"

"They don't ask questions, and neither do we," my father interjects. "Now help me up."

I toil and tug at him as he raises himself up the steps by the railing. He takes each step as slow as a snail. Even though it takes a lot of blood, sweat, and tears, we make it up.

When we finally get to the top, I breathe out ragged breaths and open the doors.

There's a hallway in front of us with lots of rooms.

We skipped right past the check-in area, just as the man said.

My father whips out his card and checks the number. "Fifty-two."

Down the hall and to the right. I put my arm under his shoulder to support him while we walk there. Only a few more steps…

When the door finally opens, I help him inside. But when I've put him down on a seat, and the door shuts behind us, I immediately exit the room again.

"Wait—"

I ignore my father's voice and peek through the hallways until I find what I'm looking for. The cleaning lady's cart and the bag filled with clothes destined for the cleaners.

When I'm sure no one is around, I rummage through the bag and fish out a white shirt that's not too dirty, along with a pair of fancy suit trousers. Nothing I'd normally ever wear, but perfect to blend in.

I blow out a sigh.

I promise to bring these back once I get to safety.

Then I head back into the room and shut the door.

My father stares at me and the clothes in my hands. "What the hell are you up to?"

I don't respond as I lock myself in the bathroom and look at the woman in the mirror. At her bloodied fingertips and stained purple dress.

I tear off the dress, ripping it at the seams until all that remains are the pieces on the floor. I wash my face and my hands under the sink, watching the blood slowly disappear down the drain. But no amount of rubbing can get rid of this smudge darkening my heart.

I clean myself off and quickly put on the clothes I stole. They don't smell that bad. Anything is better than that dress bought with lives.

When I'm ready, I exit the bathroom and stand there for a moment while my father glares at me.

"Just a change of clothes? That's it?" he asks. "Where did you get them?"

"I stole them," I say. "But I'll bring them back once we're in a safer space, I promise."

He simply makes a *hmpf* sound, and I recognize it from when he always used to berate me. But now, my father's judgment is the least of my worries.

Besides, it's not like he didn't make a business out of stealing. He has no right to judge.

I collapse onto the bed and stay there for a while. Just

breathing. Just … existing.

And then the tears come.

"Are you crying?" my father mutters. "Jesus, Aurora. We made it. Be happy." He laughs.

"We did, yes," I reply, gazing at him with tearstained eyes. "But *he* didn't."

"Who?" My father raises his brow, but the ire on my face finally makes him realize. "That Beast?"

He says his name like it's something vile.

Suddenly, he hisses as he moves around in the chair, and I sit up to look at him.

"Fuck, it hurts," he growls, touching the open wounds on his legs and arms.

I wipe away my tears, get off the bed, and rummage around in the room, opening all the closets. I even look in the bathroom until I find what I'm looking for: a first-aid kit.

I carry it to my father and kneel before him so I can bandage his leg. I don't say anything at all, even though he looks at me like I should. But I have absolutely nothing to say to him.

"Why do you even care at all about that Beast?" he asks.

I fixate the bandage with some tape. "Because he deserved to survive too."

He rolls his eyes. "That *thing* was nothing but a killer."

"That *thing* was a man with a beating heart," I say, standing up in front of him. "And he was a better man than you'll ever be."

I blink away the tears, refusing to cry in front of my father as I throw everything back into the box and chuck it onto the table. Then I lie down in the bed and bury my face into the pillow.

It's been so long since I last felt a semblance of humanity, and this bed right here gives me so much of it. Something Beast didn't have for years on end.

Until he met me.

That one night we had in the hotel room must've been a rare experience.

"So you're just going to lie there?" my father asks.

I don't know what to say.

I'm just trying not to die from sorrow.

Because when I think of Beast lying there in a pool of his own blood, shot down like his life meant nothing, all I want to do is scream until my lungs cave in on me.

"You really want to ignore your own father?"

"Yes," I mutter, tasting my salty tears as they roll down my cheeks. "Yes, pretending you don't exist is easier than knowing you're here."

Even though he's alive, even though I just gave him some first aid, even though he's my father, I don't want anything to do with him right now.

My father makes a *pfft* sound and turns around in his chair. "Fine. I'll sleep here for the night."

I ignore his obvious attempt at guilt-tripping me. I've felt so guilty all this time while I was in that cell beneath Lex's mansion, and for what? So my father could tell me to my face he never even wanted me? That he'd easily exchange me to save his life? That I'm … a monster?

The mere thought makes me bury my face in my pillow again, wishing I could unsee the world. Unsee my own body and my own hands that have destroyed so much in this life.

I lean up only to look at my own deformity.

I used to see so much hope when I still had my gloves.

But now … all I see is carnage.

Straight from these fingertips that chose to save my father …

At the cost of the life of the only man who sacrificed everything to save me.

Two

Aurora

After a few hours, I abruptly wake from a dreamless, restless sleep to my father touching my shoulder.

"Aurora. I'm hungry. We need to fix something."

I frown, sighing out loud as I'm still struggling to wake up. "How? I don't have money."

"I don't know," he hisses. "Go out there and see what you can do."

Why do I always have to do everything?

I roll my eyes, but then my stomach growls too.

Grumbling, I push myself off the pillow, get up, and walk into the bathroom to splash cold water on my face. Then I open the door. There's a cart in the hallway of another hotel guest that never touched his dinner.

Could I? Should I?

What other choice do I have?

Looking around to make sure no one's watching, I quickly sneak toward it and push it into our room, then lock the door.

I know it's bad. I know it's wrong.

But my stomach is growling, and I need to survive.

I pull off the plastic covers and look at all the delicious food. A steak, potatoes, cheese-covered broccoli, some chips, and a chocolate dessert.

"Well, it's not much," my father complains.

"It's something," I retort, frowning at him.

I grab the cutlery and cut into the meat, but my father eyes me down. "I'd like that."

I roll my eyes. "Fine, I don't care." And I grab a piece of broccoli instead. The taste is divine and almost makes me want to cry. I haven't had a decent meal in ages. Most I ever got in the cell was bread, water, and sometimes a bit of soup. This has texture and taste, and actual effort was put into it.

And it almost reminds me of home.

Or at least … what I remember of it before it was stolen from me.

Before my father tainted the mere memory of it.

"Give me the fork and knife," he says, hurriedly snatching it from my fingers so he can cut into the meat and devour it.

I grab the broccoli and sit down onto the bed, eating it in silence while he stands in front of the cart, refusing to move.

I'm happy with my little cup of broccoli.

And when it's all finished, I rush back to the cart to take some potatoes too.

"I split it equally," I say when my father looks at me with disdain again.

He grumbles. "Well, I'm hungry."

My lip twitches. I am too.

"Do you even know what I went through?" he asks, chewing on one of them. "I was tied down and beaten for days."

He doesn't seem to even remotely care to ask me how I was treated as he continues shoveling them inside. So I take what's mine and jump back on the bed, eating as fast as possible before he tries to steal some away from me.

Hunger makes one do strange things.

When everything's gone, all that's left is dessert. And we both eye it like hungry vultures.

"You had the meat," I mutter.

He raises his brow. "So? You had the broccoli."

"I'm your daughter," I say through gritted teeth.

Does he even care?

Suddenly, he chucks the little container at me. "Fine. Have it. Ungrateful little kid."

I frown and stare at it, refusing to take the lid off. Even if it tasted like a bite out of heaven's clouds, it still wouldn't manage to erase the sour aftertaste of his inability to care about his daughter's needs.

All I am to him is a burden. Something annoying that gets in his way.

And I can't believe I never saw it before when we still lived under one roof.

I lie down in the bed and place the container on the nightstand.

"Aren't you going to eat it?" my father asks as he sits in the chair.

"I'm saving it for later."

"What a waste," he grumbles.

A waste.

That's how he's always seen it.

How he's always treated me.

So I sigh and grab the chocolate, ripping off the lid just so I can spoon it out with my finger. Not because it's a waste to let it sit, or because I'm so damn hungry I can't resist … but because I refuse to let him ruin this too.

The taste is delicious and everything I expected it to be. And it almost makes me cry.

I wish Beast could have a bite.

I wish I could let him know I was safe.

And I wish I could just … hold him tight.

As tears well up in my eyes, I put down the cup and slide underneath the blanket, throwing my head down onto the pillow so I don't have to think about it anymore.

But even if I let my mind wander as I fall into a deep

slumber, my dreams always go back to him.

BANG!

The gun goes off right in front of me.

A bullet enters his skull.

Blood splashes all around me.

And I scream so loud my eardrums feel like they're pierced.

Shrieking, I sit up straight in bed, covered in sweat. I throw the blanket off and stare at the wall for a while, trying to regain my bearings. I don't know how much time has passed, but it feels like everything went by in a flash. I was right there in that warehouse again, in front of that chair, but instead of my father being strapped to it … it was Beast.

And I watched as the gun tore a hole into his forehead.

My hand instantly covers my mouth as I swallow a panicked whimper.

My father's snoring tears my eyes away from the wall. He's fast asleep in the chair, mouth half-open, a fly resting on his bandaged leg. The stench of food gone bad and old blood and dirt fills the room and makes my stomach flip over.

I run to the bathroom and throw up in the toilet until I'm empty, and everything hurts. There goes the food I needed so badly.

I flush, but the sound of water rushing past me only makes the tears roll faster, harder, uncontrollably. I sink to the floor and lie on the tiles, staring at the light up above. And I wish now, more than ever before, that I could've taken Beast with me.

That I'd be able to turn back time and fight with him by his side.

That I could've saved him instead of my father.

I cover my eyes with my hands, unable to look at the world, let alone myself, for even thinking about it. Hiccups make my breathing unsteady, so I sit up to try to regain control. But my breathing is irregular, and every breath feels like a stab to the heart.

I ran because Beast told me to, because he wanted to give me the gift of freedom, but now that I'm here safely in this hotel, I feel like I made the wrong choice.

I left him there to die.

BANG!

I can still hear the gunshot ricochet in my head. Over and over again, like a song on repeat. But this song only plays in my nightmares, and I want it to stop.

Is he really dead?

The thought makes my throat clamp up.

Could it be true?

My eyes water again.

I have to know. I need to know if he's dead or not.

Suddenly, the door to the bathroom opens up, and my father stares at me in the doorway.

"What are you doing here?" he asks, apparently up on his feet again. "You need to sleep. You'll need the energy for the coming days."

"I don't care," I mutter.

He snorts. "What do you mean, *you don't care?*"

He looks at me like I've gone insane.

Maybe I have.

"I don't care if I have energy or not." Tears roll down my cheeks. "I don't care anymore. About anything." It's all coming out now. "I left him to die."

My father stares at me for a moment as if he's trying to figure out who I'm talking about, but then it finally clicks.

"That Beast was too busy mauling everyone," my father replies with disdain. "You're lucky you escaped."

"He *let* me escape," I bark back. "You don't understand. I know that man. This was not an easy choice to make for him."

"What could you possibly know about him or anything else?" He frowns. "You've barely even seen the outside world."

"Because you wouldn't let me!" I yell. "And all these years I thought it was because you wanted to protect me. From the bullies. From the harshness of the outside world." I take in a deep breath. "But that wasn't it, was it? You just wanted to pretend I didn't exist."

His nostrils flare, and he briefly looks away, like he can't even stomach looking at me.

So I scream and raise my hands. "Look at me!"

When he does, there's only regret in his eyes. He can't even look at the scars on my hands.

"This is what it's all about. Me. You wanted to fix me, and you spent all of your money and Lex's money to get it done. But it didn't work. And now you blame me."

"I did everything for you!" he says through gritted teeth. "All my hard work, all the pain, all the suffering. *For you*!"

His words hurt.

"And you're not even a little bit grateful," he growls.

I shake my head, incensed he'd even say that. "I was …" I reply under my breath. "And I tried so hard not to break." I look up into his eyes that are filled with as much hatred as I feel in my soul right now. "Do you even know what they did to me? Where they locked me up?"

He doesn't respond so I continue.

"In a tiny cell underneath the house. No bed. No food. No sunlight."

He swallows. "Thanks to that Beast."

"You know who else was there with me in that darkness?" I grind my teeth. "*That* Beast."

My misery has turned into an uncontrollable anger I don't recognize in myself.

"He brought me back to Lex because he would've died if he didn't. He was as much a prisoner as me," I say, and I get up from the floor. "But you … you left me in that cell to die. Not once did you attempt to save me."

He merely grits his teeth, like he can't even stomach a reply or show me even a semblance of regret.

"All those things you said in that warehouse …" I mutter to myself, but I know he heard.

"I said and did what I had to, to survive. Just like you," he scoffs, offended.

"You called me a monster," I say.

My father snorts like he can't fathom even thinking about it, let alone saying it out loud.

But he did.

He called me a monster because he thinks I'm ugly.

And I won't forget.

"We both did everything we could to live. You did some awful things too. I heard Lex. He said you told him you'd help him find me."

My eyes widen, and I quickly march past him.

"Don't you fucking run away from me now, Aurora," he barks behind me.

"I'm done with this conversation," I retort. I grab one of the keys and stuff it into my pocket.

"Where are you going?" he asks, trying to block my way, but I shove him aside.

He instantly hisses from the pain in his wounds, but I don't care.

All the respect I once had for him has vanished.

"Out."

***

I don't even think about the consequences, as I head right back to the same warehouse where my father was caught and almost killed.

I know it's dangerous as hell, and that I'm doing something really, really stupid. But I need to know if he's okay. If he's … alive.

I swallow back the nerves as I make my way across the street, glaring at everyone who even dares to cross my path. I don't know who can be trusted, so I opt not to trust anyone at all. Everyone could be a spy, a guard, or a friend of Lex's.

I slither through an alley and come out in the same port where all the warehouses are. I don't remember exactly what warehouse it was, but I can retrace my steps.

When I pass the alley where I found my father behind the dumpster, I know I'm on the right track.

My heart begins to palpitate as I make my way along the docks, carefully checking my surroundings to make sure no one sees me. I don't want to get caught by Lex's henchmen.

When someone passes by, I hide behind a metal container and wait until there's no more sound before I continue.

I sneak across the pavement and along the sides of the buildings until I finally reach the one I remember. The mere sight of its doors makes my skin crawl, but I still go inside. Every step I take makes my heart beat faster and faster. I look around again to make sure no one's there, but it's the middle of the night, and it would be strange for anyone to be working now. Besides, this warehouse is owned by my father. Or was, before Lex ransacked it.

Lots of the boxes filled with marihuana, money, guns, and other drugs are gone now. They emptied the place. The only thing left is that same chair in the middle of the warehouse.

And blood.

Lots of blood.

I push away the nerves and go to my knees, checking out the locations of the puddles. Most of them I remember from the attacks Beast made on the guards. But one of them … right in front of the chair … that's new.

I shudder in place as I touch the blood, and my stomach immediately wants to flip over again.

He was here.

This is where Lex … shot him.

I swallow back down the bile.

Where is he?

I get up and check the office, but no one is there either. Just a bunch of boxes and papers spilled all over the floor.

"Beast?" I mutter, knowing full well that making any sound is dangerous, but it doesn't seem like anyone is around to hear.

I head into the bathroom in the back, but that's empty too, as are the storage units scattered all over the warehouse.

"Beast?!" I say, this time louder than before.

Still no response.

This place … It's empty.

Completely devoid of any human presence.

Like no one was ever here.

And it makes it hard to breathe.

"Beast …" I say as I sink to the floor, feeling like the world is slowly caving in on me.

I thought I'd find him here. That he'd be lying here in a puddle of his own blood. Dead.

Instead, it's almost like he never existed at all.

All that remains of him is a bloodstain, spreading like poison across the concrete floor.

Where did they take him?

Tears form in my eyes.

I came here because I needed to know the truth. If he was even alive at all.

But now I'll never know.

And I didn't even get a chance to say goodbye.

***

I have to physically drag myself toward our room in the shoddy hotel. But the second I open the door and step one foot inside, my father is immediately up in my face.

"Where were you? Did anyone follow you?"

"What? No, of course not," I reply, passing by him.

"How do you know? Did you even check before you came back?" He pushes me away and glares into the hallway like a hawk before shutting the door behind me. "What did you even do out there?"

"What's with all the questions?" I reply.

He grabs my shoulders and shakes me around like a doll. "Answer me, Aurora!"

I'm flabbergasted. It's been a long time since he put his hands on me like this.

I used to cower in fear and cry when he would … but I'm not that same girl I used to be.

I shove him away. "I went back to the warehouse."

His eyes slowly widen, like he realizes I made his worst fear a reality.

Suddenly, he bursts into a rage, clutching my collar. "Are you out of your goddamn mind?"

"Let go of me." I slap his hand off my clothes, and I turn around and walk toward the window to gaze outside. I don't even know what I'm looking at, but anywhere is better than having to look at my father. "I did what I had to do."

"Do what? Throw yourself at the enemy?" he says through gritted teeth. "After all that effort to escape?"

"I needed to know if he was alive!" I yell. Turning to face him, I show him all the rage coiled up inside me.

For a moment, he simply stares at me. "He's literally a killer who tried to murder both of us, and you care whether he's even alive?"

"He's the *only* reason we still breathe," I spit back, taking ample time to articulate my words because I want my father to take them seriously. "He deserved far more than what he got."

Suddenly, the door handle is jiggled, and we both fall silent. Instantly.

My eyes are drawn to the door. So are my father's.

The fumbling doesn't stop.

Someone's here.

Three

Aurora

Anxiety floods my body.

I take a step back, bumping into the window.

"They found us!" my father whisper-yells at me.

He quietly crosses the floor and picks up a lamp from the desk, holding it up like some sort of weapon.

And when the lock is finally pushed off, the door swings open, and a man storms inside, eyes like the devil. I shriek as my father chucks the lamp at him and misses.

The man charges at my father with a knife, but my father catches his wrist and holds him back. But his wounds are grave, and his body still too frail to handle the attack. He's losing ground.

In a panic, I search for anything I can use, but all I find is a flower vase. Without thinking, I pick it up and approach the man from the back. They're fighting for power near the bed, and all the pieces of furniture are shoved aside. My father tumbles over the bed, a knife almost in his face.

I slam the vase into the back of the man's head as hard as I can.

It shatters into a million tiny pieces, and the man falls right on top of my father. The knife tumbles to the floor.

But the man swiftly turns around to face me, the fury on his face terrifying.

He throws a punch, and I duck for cover, picking up a shard on the way.

Right as he comes down, I jump back and hold the shard in front of me like a knife.

"Stay back!" I yell.

"Oh, you gonna play the big girl now?" he mutters.

His voice makes me tremble on my feet.

I recognize it.

He's one of Lex's guards.

"Come at me, then," he growls, throwing punch after punch.

I tiptoe sideways, trying to avoid his fist, but I'm not trained, and when I slip up, he punches me right in the gut.

Oof.

My lungs feel like they got run over by a truck, and I buck and heave.

"You thought you could run from us?" The guard

laughs. "Bad idea."

Suddenly, my father rises from the bed and smacks the guard on the head with a thick book he'd found lying by the table.

The man is slapped sideways headfirst into the wooden wardrobe next to the bed, allowing me to step away.

My father gets off the bed and punches the guy, but the guard grabs his fist in midair and pushes him back. They struggle for power, and my father is definitely on the losing end.

My hand that holds the shard begins to quake.

I don't have much time.

Make a choice.

Just do it.

Do it now.

I don't think as I ram the shard into the man's back.

He roars out in pain, scratching at his skin to try to get it out.

"You fucking bitch!"

He turns around and punches me.

Dizzy, I fall to the floor, unable to keep my balance, and a sharp pain makes me groan.

One of the shards has lodged itself into my abdomen.

When I touch it and look at my hands, there's blood.

Oh God.

My father throws himself at the guard, hanging around his neck and biting his ear.

The man growls in pain and chucks my father forward

over his head, slamming him into the floor so hard I can hear the air leave his body.

My father doesn't move anymore.

Then the guard focuses his attention on me.

My pupils dilate, and I immediately begin to crawl away from him.

Too late.

"I should've killed you when I had the chance." His shrill voice sounds like nails on a chalkboard.

I head for the knife he dropped, but before I can reach it, he grabs my hair and drags me up. It hurts so bad my eyes begin to sting with tears.

"But I'll definitely enjoy being the one to make you both suffer," he growls.

I've already suffered enough.

In a blind rage, I grasp the shard and pull it out of my own flesh.

And when he turns me around, I jab it straight into his eye.

One. Two. Three steps and he falls, wailing in agony, straight into the corner of the nightstand. His head splits open, and blood pours out. The one leftover eye slowly grows vacant. And then he breathes his last breath.

I stare at him for a moment, wondering if he'll come back alive like a zombie and eat us all. But none of that happens.

I take a couple of deep breaths, trying to tell myself it's fine.

But it's not.

I killed a man.

I actually killed a human being.

But the worst part is … I don't feel any different.

I should. Taking a life should not be this easy. Nor should I be happy.

But I am. I'm so goddamn happy I survived another day.

Is it wrong to feel this way?

Is this … is this what Beast experienced whenever he killed?

I swallow down the lump in my throat.

When I'm finally convinced the guard will not get up again, I breathe a sigh of relief and push myself up from the floor. I lean up, but the wound in my stomach plays up, and I hiss in pain.

Someone else does too.

My eyes immediately turn toward the sound, and my heart stops racing the second I spot my father moaning in the corner. For a second, I thought another guard would come to get us.

"Fuck me …" he groans in pain.

I get up slowly, grabbing the bed to help myself stand. The wound isn't deep, but it definitely needs stitches.

"Check if he's dead," my father says between ragged breaths.

Frowning, I reply, "You do it." And I head into the bathroom to find the first-aid kit. There's a tiny needle and thread inside. Not perfect, but it'll have to do.

I sit on the counter and lift my shirt to look at myself in the mirror. The wound looks gnarly and oozes blood. I grab the tiny alcohol wipes and clean the wound, hissing with pain. Then I lean in with the needle.

C'mon, Aurora. You can do this.

I push the pointy end into my skin and bite down on my lip as I push it through again and again, sealing the wound slowly.

God, the things I've had to do since I got captured.

Old Aurora wouldn't ever have believed it.

"What are you doing in there?" my father asks.

"Taking care of my wound," I reply when I'm finished.

I put on a bandage and make sure everything looks okay before I lower my shirt and get off the counter. It feels better already, but it'll take a while to heal.

"What wound?"

I step out of the door and look at my father. He's sitting in the broken seat, taking in our ravaged room.

"A shard lodged itself into my belly," I say when he looks at me.

"Oh …" He looks away again.

"*Oh?*" I mutter. "That's all you're going to say?"

"Well, it's your own fault," he points out.

My eyes widen, and my face scrunches up. "*What?*"

"You should be happy you're still alive." He clears his throat, rubbing his wounds.

"Well you should be too," I quip. "I saved us both."

He stares at the dead body, sighing out loud.

"You killed him," he retorts.

"He tried to kill us first," I say, making a face.

He turns to look at me. "Well, now we have to run again. They'll surely come looking for him."

I frown. "How do you even know?"

"Because you brought them to our doorstep!" He's suddenly so enraged that I don't know what to do with it.

"I checked. No one was following m—"

"They found us!" he barks. "It's too late for excuses. You shouldn't have gone out. Look at what kind of shit it got us into."

He's cruel beyond words. "I did my best."

"Not good enough," he says through gritted teeth. "And even if they didn't follow us here, there's no way the hotel will accept this. They don't do body disposals. Now we'll never be welcome here again." He points at the man like he's mere trash. "Where are we going to fucking sleep now, Aurora?"

"You're acting like all of this is my fault, like I shouldn't have killed the guy. But what else was I supposed to do?" I swallow back the tears.

"Keep him alive. Maybe I could've negotiated with him after we'd strapped him down."

"Like we even stood a chance! We could barely take him with the two of us. He almost choked and killed you!" I yell back, unable to keep the emotions at bay. "I did what I had to do to save us!" I'm right up in his face now. "I was stabbed by a piece of broken glass, and you don't even care."

He grinds his teeth, but the lack of words speaks volumes.

I can't listen to another minute of this.

I turn around and head to the door.

"Where are you going now?" he scoffs. "You don't even have your gloves on. What if people see?"

That's all he's ever cared about.

Appearances.

Reputation.

Perfection.

Something I'll never be in his eyes.

Something I wished so badly I could be to my papa.

But the more time I spend with him now, the more I'm beginning to realize … the papa I thought I knew only existed in my mind as a cruel dream that would never be a reality.

I open the door.

"Don't you think of going back to that warehouse again! What if more of them follow, huh? You want that on your conscience?"

"Don't worry," I reply, refusing to even grant him one more look. "You won't be bothered anymore."

And I slam the door shut as harshly as the door to my heart.

Four

Aurora

I'm cold. Icy cold. But I try not to let it get to me as I roam the streets, looking for a safe space to sleep.

I don't know where I'm going or even where I'm at.

All I know is that this is the port city of the Netherlands, Rotterdam, and there's nothing here that I recognize from home.

It's the middle of the night and frigid out here. I hide my hands inside my shirt, not to keep people from looking but because I'm so freaking cold. I don't have a coat to keep me warm, but I don't want to steal. I've already taken these clothes off some unsuspecting stranger, and I felt terrible.

And the more I wander, the more I feel like I'm losing

myself. My body.

As though I'm floating above myself and looking down, pitying the woman strolling the streets, searching for a place to go. A place of comfort. A place to call home.

But there is no such thing anymore.

Home and everything I associated it with was nothing more than a fairy tale.

A dark lie I'd told myself in order to cope with the horrible world.

A world in which I was born but never wanted.

A world in which everything would've been better if I had … ceased to exist.

Suddenly, my stomach contracts, and I hold my hand in front of my belly. It hurts. Badly.

What if …?

My eyes widen.

No, it can't be.

I have to know.

I turn around and around, trying to find a shop, but there are only clothing stores and luxury boutiques.

Shit, I have to find a pharmacy. Fast.

I follow a woman who just passed me and stop in front of her. "Sorry, excuse me, ma'am, can you help me? I need a pharmacy."

She frowns, wary of me, so I swiftly tuck my hands into my pocket. "A pharmacy?"

"Yeah, for medicine and stuff."

"Oh. Apotheek." She points at a street a few feet away

from this one. "There's one around there, to the left."

"Thanks!" I say, and I rush off.

I head to the street she pointed at and find a weird store I've never been to but recognize from television commercials. I quickly go inside and search until I find the aisle I'm looking for.

I stare up at the product shelf, wondering what I need. I've never done this before, and the thought is quite daunting.

Especially when it dawns on me that I have literally zero money.

I grab one of the boxes that says it has an early detection and look at the price tag. It's fifteen euros.

What do I do?

Do I just steal it?

I gaze around at the employees and customers, but they're all too busy buying and selling stuff at the counter to even notice me. My conscience is weighing on me, but I still shove the package into my pocket and pull my shirt over it, praying they won't notice.

With sweat drops forming on my face, I make my way to the exit, looking around the store like normal customers do when they're just looking without buying. But when I get to the exit, my entire body begins to shake.

BEEP! BEEP!

Uh-oh.

Without thinking, I run off as fast as I can while the employees rush out of the store after me.

"Stop!" They yell, but I ignore them.

A pang of guilt shoots through my body. I don't want to steal, but I have no other choice.

If I had the money, I'd pay them.

And maybe, if I make it out of this hell alive, I'll pay them back … one day.

But for now, I keep running, past the point where my legs can carry me until I can physically feel them caving in on me.

When I'm sure no one is following me anymore, I stop right in front of a train station.

Everything hurts.

I bend over and take a few much-needed breaths.

But when I open my eyes, I find exactly what I need to make this happen. Fifty euro cents stuck between the tiles of the pavement.

A smile spreads on my lips as I fish it out and clean it up a little. It's not a lot, but it's all I need right now.

I head into the train station, ignoring everyone's looks as I push the fifty cents into a box and go into the toilet, locking myself inside.

It stinks like old piss, but even that is better than the stench of blood I still so vividly remember from the day before.

I place some paper on the toilet and fish the package from my pocket, staring at it once more before I lower my trousers and sit down.

I close my eyes for a second and breathe out another

breath.

Then I take it out and pee over the stick that's inside.

I flush and wait, nauseous just from the mere idea of having to wait for the results.

The seconds feel like hours.

A drop of sweat rolls down onto the stick.

But no extra line appears.

I let go of a giant breath and slowly begin to smile. Then laugh. Then cry.

All at once.

Because even though I'm happy I'm not pregnant, that I'm not carrying … an actual baby.

It was his.

I would have been.

I would have had something of his.

Something to remind me he was once alive.

Even though this would've been the worst time to have a baby.

Sucking in a breath, I wipe away the tears, then chuck the stick into the trash. I rush out the door and slam it shut behind me. I need to get away from there, that toilet, and that stick as fast as possible.

Storming away from the train station, I march on until I no longer feel the sting of my own tears on my cheeks and my heart and body feel numb.

I pause for a moment when my muscles can't take it anymore.

An alleyway next to me calls to me, and even though I

know I shouldn't, I can't help but walk inside. Out there on the streets, I feel watched. Unsafe. But here, behind all the rubble and in the dark, no one will be able to find me.

It's a darkness akin to the cell I'd grown so used to.

Now it all feels like a distant memory.

I sink down against the building and watch the people walk by, oblivious that I'm even here, stuck in a place between.

Two sparkling eyes suddenly catch my attention a few feet away as they blink. A man moves around on the ground, croaking and clearing his throat as he sits straight. "Hoi meisje."

That sounded Dutch, and I definitely don't speak Dutch. Although I've lived here for ages, my papa never let me mingle with any of the locals. And the school I briefly attended was also for English students. So I have no clue what to say.

"Um … hi," I reply.

"Geen Nederlands?"

"I only speak English," I reply.

"Interesting. And American too, right?" he asks.

How does he know?

"Your accent gives it away," he muses, smiling.

He shuffles around on the ground, and I realize I may have intruded on something.

"Sorry, am I bothering you? I can leave," I mutter, and I immediately get up.

"No, no, it's fine. Stay for as long as you want," he says.

So I sit down again slowly, wondering what I'm supposed to do.

"So what's a girl like you doing out here in a dark alley?" he asks.

I gulp down the nerves. "I just … I don't know."

"Hmm," he muses. "Yeah, same." And he laughs. "You don't have to tell me anything. I'm only trying to be friendly, that's all."

"Thanks," I say, smiling too.

"What's your name?" he asks.

"Aurora." I'm not going to give my last name to anyone. Maybe not ever again.

I'm not proud of it and don't think I'll ever be.

"Mine's Dirk," he says, and he offers me his hand.

I lean in to give him a handshake. "Nice to meet you, Dirk."

We exchange more friendly smiles, and I get the sense this man's not as scary as I thought he'd be when I laid eyes on him moments ago.

"Are you here often?"

He chuckles and grabs a box from the pile of trash beside him. "Oh, girl, I live here." He makes it sound like a joke, but it's not funny at all. Not to me.

"I'm sorry," I reply.

"Oh, don't be. I've made my peace long ago," he says. "I know where I belong." He leans back against the wall, closes his eyes, and takes a deep breath. "I enjoy my freedom."

"Hmm, I wish I could see things that way."

Just one of his eyes opens. "Why can't you?"

"I'm … on the run from my own mistakes."

I'm not going to tell a stranger about everything I've been through.

He waves a hand around. "Everyone makes mistakes. Doesn't make it impossible to enjoy freedom."

I gaze around at his carton shack amongst the rubble. "This? This is freedom to you?" I mutter.

"Of course," he says. "No rules, nothing to watch over, no bills to pay." He grins. "I prefer this over work any day of the week."

I've never looked at it that way. I've been so secluded from the real world that I never realized it could be just as good if not better than the life my father was building for me.

Maybe this … this is the kind of freedom I should want.

"Freedom … freedom of the mind," Dirk muses, almost as if he's floating off into his own brain.

And it only makes me smile.

I always thought the people living on the streets were worse off than I was, but now I'm not so sure anymore.

The rain suddenly begins to pitter-patter, and I look at the gray sky. It's about to break loose. And with nowhere to stay or go, I'm going to get soaking wet soon.

"Here." Dirk holds out a shoddy, half-broken umbrella to me. "For the rain."

"Um … Thanks," I reply, caught off guard.

While I raise it up high, he rummages around in his stash until he finds what he's looking for. "Ah! I knew I had another one."

He holds up a giant box made of plastic, big enough to hold a tiny human. Maybe even big enough for me if I pulled my legs up.

He places it near the building right next to me and pats it down, then throws in a ragged blanket he fishes out of his stash. "It's not much, but it's something."

I look at it, wondering what he means.

"Made you a bed," he muses.

"A bed?" I mutter, flabbergasted. "For me?"

"I just thought you might need a place. I mean, people don't normally talk to me, so I figured you were in a rough spot just like me."

Tears well up in my eyes from the sheer kindness this stranger is showing me. "I can't pay you."

"I don't need money," he says, laughing. "But if you don't want it, that's fine too. I won't force you to stay."

"No, no," I say, struggling to keep my voice from fluctuating. "Of course, I'd love to."

"Why are you crying?" he asks.

I brush aside the tears. "I'm just grateful." I smile at him as I get up and huddle up in the tiny carton house. "Thank you."

He smiles back in the gentlest of ways. "You're welcome. And feel free to stay as long as you'd like. I quite enjoy having someone to talk to once in a while."

I look up at him, the smile on his face something unfamiliar to me. Even though my spirit is broken, this man manages to capture what's left of my heart.

I hug my legs, not giving a shit that he can see my deformed hands.

Not once has he looked at my fingers or asked why they are the way they are.

Papa always told me the world would be cruel, but this man has shown me kindness, and nothing but grace and decency is in his eyes. Something I thought was severely lacking in my life before.

One thing that wasn't lacking—cruelty.

The kind my father and Lex candidly dished out.

And even though I left that hotel room in tears, I'm no longer crying them over my father. I refuse to. He doesn't deserve these tears.

So I smile until all of them have disappeared, listening to the rain pitter-patter onto the carton while the man in front of me slowly crawls onto the floor and closes his eyes.

And I watch him fall asleep with a kind of peace I've rarely ever seen.

A peace I wish I could feel deep down in my heart.

But I don't know if I could ever reach that point.

That point when I know life will be okay.

Not without Beast.

Five

Aurora

When a bright light enters my eyes, I jolt up and down, my head bumping into the carton box. Blinking rapidly, I gaze at my surroundings. The sun is out and bursting with radiance.

Did I … sleep?

A yawn immediately leaves my mouth.

It wasn't an amazing sleep, but apparently, I felt safe enough to doze off.

"Well, good morning," Dirk says with a happy smile. "Sleep well?"

I stretch out a little. "Okay-ish."

"Ah, you'll get used to it." He waves it off as he gets off

the floor and starts rummaging in his stuff again. "I don't have cash, but I definitely have some leftover food from yesterday if you want some."

Even though my stomach is growling, I'm not looking to get a stomach bug right now. "No, thanks. I'm not hungry."

He holds up a stale half-eaten sandwich. "You sure?"

I nod, smiling. "Of course. Take it."

He sits down and happily munches on the food. "Tastes better the next day." He laughs in such a funny way that it makes me giggle. "Everything is better the next day."

"You really think so?" I ask.

"Yeah. I mean, what's the worst that can happen?" he muses, gazing around. "That I become homeless?"

I smile. "That's a positive outlook."

"Exactly," he says, winking.

"I wish I could see it the same way," I say.

"Do you have family?" he asks.

"Yes," I say, but I quickly add, "Well, I did."

"What happened?" he asks. "It's fine if you don't want to answer. I won't pry."

"It's okay. I just needed to run away."

"I understand. I ran away lots of times back when I was your age," he replies.

I look up into his eyes. "You have family you left behind too?"

He nods and takes another bite of his sandwich. "Oh yeah, I actually just visited my daughter this morning while you were still sleeping. She works at a small local clinic."

I sit up straight.

He was gone while I was asleep all by myself?

What if someone had mugged me?

I have nothing of value to steal, but still, the thought of being alone out in the streets frightens me.

"I don't know what was going on at that clinic, but it sure wasn't the usual kind of business."

"What do you mean?" I ask.

He takes a big bite and chews while speaking. "Lots of big guys in suits and blacked-out cars in the parking lot, and when I went inside, they were all sitting in the waiting room, staring at a single door." He shivers. "Creepy if you ask me."

My eyes widen.

Could it be …?

I immediately crawl out of the carton box and get up.

"What's wrong?"

"Where is that clinic?"

"Uh … five streets farther up ahead, then the last to the left. Not far from here."

"Did you see anyone come in with huge scars?" I ask, panicked.

He shakes his head. "I don't know. I didn't see much other than those men. They were already sitting there by the time I came in."

"I have to go," I mutter. "Thank you so much for letting me stay."

"Wait, what? Where?" he replies, but I've already run

out of the alley and down onto the street.

I know I didn't say a proper goodbye, but there's no more time.

If I don't go now, I might not be there on time to find out if my hunch is true.

If the people at that clinic are who I think they are … Lex's guards … then the person in that room they're watching might be Beast.

I run across the pavement, bumping into people and apologizing profusely before I run off again. Some seem upset I don't pay attention, but my focus is on one thing and one thing only: I have to know if he's still alive.

Could Lex have brought him there?

Beast was important to him, after all. Lex only saw him as a weapon, but he went to such lengths to keep him imprisoned, so he must still be of use.

Right?

He wouldn't let him die, right?

My heart is racing as I cross street after street, paying little attention to the lights even though I know it's wrong. Passersby look at me like I've lost my mind, but I don't care.

If I don't get there in time, he might be gone before I know the truth.

C'mon, c'mon, c'mon!

I force my legs to go faster, despite the pain. The only thing keeping me going right now is pure adrenaline as I turn to the left and the clinic comes into view.

All I can think about is finding Beast.

The man whose name I don't even know, but whose presence and power are still cemented in my mind. Because he was the only man who ever cared about me and chose my needs over himself. Over his own life.

And if there's even a remote chance he might still be alive, I have to know.

I have to be there for him like he was for me.

I have to save him.

When I finally get to the building, I run through the front door and pause to look around. Some of the clinic's employees stop to stare because I come running in so violently.

I adjust my posture, hide my hands in my pockets, and saunter to the front desk. "Hi."

"Kan ik je helpen?" the lady says.

Oh shit, more Dutch people. Of course.

After all these years, I'm still not used to it.

But I guess that's what you get when your father rarely lets you out.

"Uh … do you speak English?" I ask.

The lady smiles awkwardly. "Of course."

I clear my throat and wait until the rest of the employees stop looking at me like I'm a threat.

"I'm looking for a patient. Wondering if he might be here."

She narrows her eyes at me. "What's the name?"

Oh. I hadn't actually thought about this before I came here.

A blush creeps onto my cheeks. "People call him Beast."

The lady in front of the desk makes a funny face. "Okay … and surname?"

"I don't have any," I reply.

I look around to make sure I don't recognize anyone. I don't want to get caught by Lex's henchmen. Even though I know what I'm doing right now could get me into trouble.

She glares at me. "And what is yours then?"

Shit. Should I answer truthfully or make up a lie?

Then I remember … Lex. His wife's name. I can use her.

"Anne," I say. "Anne De Vos."

The woman licks her lips and checks something on her computer.

Has Lex's wife never come here?

I hope not, or she'll surely know I'm not her.

"The man I'm looking for is kind of huge. He's got a lot of scars," I say, trying not to panic. "Hard to miss."

It only makes her narrow her eyes even further. "Well, since you're *his* wife," she murmurs, rolling her eyes as she taps onto the keyboard. "I may be able to make an exception to our rules here."

I'm amazed at my ability to lie as I smile through this awkward conversation. But the moment someone dressed in all black appears from a tiny hallway in the back, I panic and turn around to face the wall.

The woman looks at me like I've lost my mind while I'm sweating profusely as the guard walks by and heads out the door.

I blow out a sigh of relief when he's gone.

"You okay, ma'am?"

"Yeah, yeah," I muse. "I'm fine. Just a little nauseous." I wave it off like it's no big deal, throwing my hair back over my shoulder. "I can't stand the look of my husband's employees."

She smiles awkwardly but still continues searching on her computer.

I don't think my lie will hold much longer.

"Ah, I see it now."

Those words make my eyes become almost glued to the screen.

"He's here?" My heart skips a beat.

"Well, he was."

The disappointment strikes almost instantly. "Oh …"

I feel like someone just ripped my heart out of my chest and stomped on it.

"I've seen him come in, but I never saw him leave," she mutters. "Not on my schedule anyway. Must've been one of my coworkers at the desk then."

I can't stop myself from asking the one question that's been on the tip of my tongue since I stepped foot inside this clinic. "Is he still alive?"

She throws me a bewildered look. "I don't know."

She checks the screen again, scrolling through the data.

My fingers dig into the counter until it almost feels like my nails pop off.

"He lost a ton of blood. Lots of doctors were involved. I wasn't there myself, but from the looks of it … probably not."

I want to scream at the top of my lungs.

Instead, all that leaves my mouth is a simple, devastating whimper.

"Can I see the room?" I ask, my voice fluctuating in tone as I attempt to keep the tears at bay.

"Sorry, lady, no can do," she replies. "I know you said you're De Vos's wife, but this is above my pay grade." She turns the monitor away and focuses on something else, signifying the end.

The end of our conversation.

The end of what little hope I had left.

The end of everything.

I turn and waltz off, my emotions blazing through me like a tornado blasting through a house, trying to find a way out. But there's nowhere to run, nowhere to hide from the debilitating sadness that overwhelms my heart as I sink to the ground behind the clinic and weep against the walls, burying my head in my hands.

He's gone.
She said it herself.
He lost so much blood … how could anyone survive?

I cry into my hands, not giving a crap that everyone can see them. All I want is one last chance. One last chance to make things right with the boy who deserved all the freedom in the world.

But I can't.

And I didn't even know his name.

"Look what we have here … A little runaway girl …" someone says. "Aurora."

When I lift my head at the sound of my name, my pupils instantly dilate.

It's one of Lex's guards.

"Gotcha."

Six

Aurora

I shriek and punch all around me, but the guard quickly has my wrists behind my back. I struggle against him as he pushes me into his body, groping me.

"Not so smart now, huh?" he growls into my ear. "You're coming with me."

"No, let go of me!" I yell, kicking and screaming.

"Dave!" another guard in the back screams.

"Here!" he replies. "I've got her!"

"Take your hands off me!" I shriek as he attempts to bind my wrists with a zip tie.

"Shut up," he growls, trying to stuff something inside my mouth, but I bite his fingers instead.

He groans in pain, blood rolling down his fingers as he tears them away. The metallic taste is disgusting, and I spit it out instantly. Can't believe Beast did this on a regular basis.

Dave spins me around on my feet. "You bitch, you bit me!" he roars and slaps me.

"Put her in the van," the other guard says.

When I finally see straight again, I fight against him as he drags me back through the alley. "No, no, no!" I say.

Not the van. Not the van!

"Stop resisting," Dave barks. "It won't get any better for you, trust me."

It won't, but I'm already at rock bottom. I have nothing left to lose except my freedom.

The freedom Beast fought so hard to grant me.

I can't go down without a fight.

So I kick and scream as loud and as hard as I can, just as he would've done if he was still here.

Somehow, someway, I manage to knee him in the balls.

He groans in pain and releases me as he bends over to heave.

I run out of the alley and into the streets, shoving one of the guards aside when he tries to tackle me. I run back inside the clinic, gazing around at the employees, begging them with my eyes to help.

"Hide me," I say, but the woman at the front desk just looks at me like she's seen a ghost.

For a moment, I stare.

Then I run into the hallway to the right with guards on

my tail. I go up a flight of stairs and another one, higher and higher, until there are no more stairs. I enter a thick, metal door, and behind it is a long hallway with only one door.

When I look over my shoulder, I can already see them running up the stairs.

No more time. Go.

I run into the only room there and gasp in shock at the sight of all the blood on the bed.

"Wha …"

"Wait! You're not supposed to go in there!" Employees yell behind me.

I quickly slam the door shut and lock it before they get inside.

Someone smashes their fists on the door, and I back away. "It's not sanitized yet! Get out of there!"

I take a few more steps back and look around for a weapon. I don't want to use it against these employees, but if they won't help me … if I have to … I will.

I grab the nearest IV pole and rid it of all the bags, then hold it out in front of me, prepared to fight like hell. Just like I told him and like he showed me.

Fight, Aurora. Fight!

"C'mon, girl, get ou—Hey! Don't push me!" a lady yelps.

More punches on the door ensue. Much louder too.

"Aurora!" My eyes widen. It's the guard. "I know you're in there. Come out. There's nowhere to run."

I turn around and look for another exit, but there is

none. Only a window.

Shit. Shit. Shit.

What am I going to do?

I step farther back and look out the window. It's way too high to jump out of, and I don't see anything to help me get down.

Are you insane? You'll never make it down alive.

Oh God, what do I do?

More punching on the door makes sweat roll down my back.

Until it all suddenly stops.

And the only thing I can hear is my own heartbeat, banging rhythmically against my ribs.

"Aurora."

The sound of his voice almost makes me drop the pole.

Lex.

The lock on the door slowly turns.

A tear forms in my eye, but I push it back and brace for impact.

CLICK!

The door unlocks. Someone lowers the handle.

My heart beats a million miles an hour.

The door slowly opens.

And the bruised-up face that appears behind gives me pure chills.

"Shouldn't have come to this clinic, Aurora," he says with a low voice. "This is the one place that serves only criminals."

"No wonder they wouldn't help …" I mutter. My eyes flutter from guard to guard, wondering which one will attack me first.

But Lex raises his hand, and all his guards stop pointing their guns at me. "I'll handle this," he tells them, then he turns to face me. "So nice to see you again." A wicked smile grows on his face.

"Stay back!" I growl, shoving the pole forward like it's a lance.

He laughs. "You've gotten feisty. Come now, put it down."

"Leave me alone!" I retort, still whipping the pole around.

"You know why I can't," he says. "You're the only connection to your father."

"He's not here," I say through gritted teeth.

"I know that," he replies, his voice lowering in tone. "So you're the next best thing I can take."

"You've destroyed *everything* I've ever cared about!" I yell in pain. "When will it ever be enough?"

He chuckles. "Everything? Hardly. Your father is still alive. So are you."

"You *killed* him. You killed Beast," I blurt out, unable to keep my feelings in check.

He frowns, but then a vicious smile slowly spreads on his face. "You seem to care an awful lot about that monster of mine …"

He takes a step forward.

"You know, when I heard they found you, I immediately came here. Lucky for you, I was only a few blocks away. Just returning in my car from a visit to this very clinic."

Oh God. Oh God.

He was right. I shouldn't have ever come here.

"Stay away!" I yell, lunging forward with my makeshift weapon.

He dodges the attack like it comes easy to him, so I hit him again and again, nearly missing the last time.

"You've gotten braver," he says. "But not brave enough."

Suddenly, he manages to grab ahold of the pole and pushes it aside so violently I lose control.

He snatches it out of my hand and throws it aside.

"You thought I needed my guards to take you?" he says. "Wrong." Every step he takes forward, I take backward. "I know how to handle a girl."

"I would rather die than have your hands on me!" I squeal.

He chuckles. "Oh, you will die … but not until after I have what I want."

The darkness in his voice makes the hairs on the back of my neck stand up.

I bump into the window and turn my head to look down.

Nowhere else to go.
What do I do?
I can't end up in his hands. I won't.

"Don't even think about it," Lex growls.

I don't think. Not even twice.

I push open the window and throw myself through it.

A sudden hand gripping my arm has me floundering halfway out the window. With a thrashing heart and a ragged breath, I'm looking at the concrete, floating between a certain death and a life not worth living.

"Don't," Lex growls. "Don't throw it all away, idiot."

"Please, let go of me," I beg. "Just let me die in peace."

Lex pulls me back in and sets me down on my feet. But not without forcefully grabbing my arm and placing a hand on my cheek. "This is what you'd choose?"

"What other choice do I have?" I say, fighting the tears.

A vicious smile slowly spreads on his face. "Your poor papa would be so distraught to see his only daughter throw herself out a window."

"My father never cared about me, only his reputation and money. He called me a monster," I say through gritted teeth, forcing the tears to stay at bay. "I have no one. No one at all. I have *nothing* left to lose."

Lex tilts his head. "Oh, you're wrong, little girl … oh so very wrong." He leans in. "Don't you want to know the truth?"

"What truth?" I mutter as he slides aside my hair.

One tiny whisper… three words … tilt my world on its axis.

"He is alive."

Seven

BEAST

Hours ago

Nightmares become me as I roll around in agony, blistering flames surrounding me everywhere. It's so hot I can barely breathe, and it feels like I've been run over by a truck.

When I open my eyes, all I see is death.

God.

I've ended up in Satan's fire.

I groan in pain as I try to move, but my arms are locked in place, tied up to something.

Have I truly died and gone to hell?

I surely belong there after all the torture I've dished out and all the lives I've taken.

Is it supposed to hurt?

And why am I exhausted?

I blink a couple of times, but all it does is make me more nauseous.

Something doesn't feel quite right.

I'm floating in and out of consciousness, struggling to even exist at all. But despite the pain and heat taking over my body, I still fight my way back.

Back to somewhere other than the fiery pits of hell.

And when I open my eyes once more, I'm in a room with white and black walls, and beneath me is a bed drenched in sweat. My sweat.

So I'm alive, after all.

But the pain … God, the fucking pain is the worst.

I move my arms, but they refuse to obey, so I turn my head to look. There are chains around my wrists.

"Wow, look. He's awake."

The voice rips through me like a knife, and I immediately turn to look where it's coming from. There's a door right in front of me.

And in it stands a man dressed in all black.

The gun in his hand sets me off.

Violence overpowers me, and I growl out loud with both pain and fury as I throw every inch of strength I have into breaking these chains that keep me down.

"Oh, shit!" the guard yells. "Call for backup. Code red."

But their voices sound dull against the shrieks in my head. Something is tormenting me, telling me to fight, fight, fight!

So I roar out loud and push myself off the bed and stomp at the guards.

"Stop him!" one of them yells. "N—"

I grab him by the throat and lift him into the air with ease, squeezing tighter and tighter until his eyes begin to bleed.

"You motherfucker!" the other guard yells, and he comes at me with a knife.

I grasp his wrist and twist it until he drops it, then bang his head into the wall until it cracks, then drop him like a fly.

He falls to the floor, blood spilling from his ears, while his buddy struggles to even breathe.

"Beast. Let go," he groans.

But I can barely even hear him.

All I hear are shrieks. Over and over.

Fight. Fight!

A girl with a picturesque face, glossy red lips, and black hair like a midnight sea comes to mind. A picture waved in front of me through the bars of what was once my home. My prison.

A prison I shared with her.

Her words ring in my ears. *Please, I don't want you to die.*

As I gasp for air, I release the guard's throat, and he drops to the floor.

Aurora.

My eyes flash with memories that pass me by in an instant.

Her father, strapped to a chair, me about to shoot him. Instead, I pointed my gun at the guards. At my owner.

I killed almost all of them.

Just so she could save her father, the man who never really loved her, and escape.

Is she alive?

My fist tightens at the idea that my owner and his henchmen could've hurt her while I was out.

Could've … killed her.

BEEP!

The loudness of the sound coming from beneath me pulls me from my thoughts.

"Where's the goddamn backup?! I need help, now!" the guard below me says with a squeaky voice. And when my eyes fall on him, he drops the walkie-talkie and crawls away from me. "No! Don't hurt me!"

Suddenly, more noise up ahead forces me to look up.

Five more guards enter the hallway, pointing their guns at me.

I remember this.

I remember this same scene happening mere hours or days ago in that same fucking warehouse where I made her run.

Only that time, it was my owner pointing his gun at me.

My hand rises to touch my back. A thick bandage covers my chest from front to back, circling me.

I'm sure the bullet went through. I can feel the stitches. The caked blood. The pain.

God, the burning pain, even now. It's like a hot poker being shoved right into my open wound. All because of *them*.

I march forward, eyes homing in.

"Stop!" the guards yell.

Or what? They'll shoot?

I'm alive.

For a reason.

He *kept* me alive.

And now I'll make him pay.

Frenzied, I stomp at them, and one of them blasts at my feet.

BANG!

I narrowly avoid the bullet.

The other one shoots right beside me, and the bullet ricochets into the wall.

They're not aiming right, which tells me they're inexperienced … or scared.

"No, no," one of them yells. "Don't get close!"

Suddenly, one of them steps forward and pushes a button in his hands.

The pain is instant, visceral, like literal lightning entering my skin. But when I touch my neck, there is no collar, nothing.

How? Why?

"Don't you fucking move an inch, or I swear to God, I'll

turn it up to the max," the guard says.

I groan in pain, suffering on the floor in agony, scratching at the back of my neck.

Something is in there, electrocuting me slowly.

And not just any kind of electrocution.

The worst, torturous pain I could ever imagine jabs me on all sides of my body.

I've felt pain before. But never this kind.

"Stop."

His voice makes me look up even though it feels like my eyes almost bulge out of my skull from the sheer amount of pain.

But then it all stops.

The agony doesn't immediately leave my body, and the memory is as vivid as it was before my near-death experience. But one thing I know for sure … the one in control is still the man I so violently hate.

"So you're awake," my owner muses, and he steps forward, looking down at me with disdain. "And already so brutal. You killed another one of my guards." He walks to the guard and kicks him, but the man doesn't move anymore. I made sure of that.

My owner makes a tsk sound. "What a waste. After all that effort I went through to keep you alive."

When I've regained enough strength, I push myself up from the floor, and the guard holding the button immediately tenses.

But my owner holds up a hand.

"No need. He will listen." He goes to his knees. "Won't you, Beast?"

"Give me one good reason," I say through gritted teeth, my voice sounding more like an animal than a human being. "I would rather *die* than obey you."

"But not in an excruciating manner, I suppose?" he muses, smiling like the devil. "I asked my technicians to upgrade the device. Give it a little edge over the old one. It hurts more, don't you think?"

I don't respond, and when I try to get up, all the muscles in my body refuse to listen. I cough, and some blood spills out onto the floor.

Even though no one touched me.

Fuck.

"What the fuck did you do to me?" I growl.

"Two things." He raises his fingers. "One. We've implanted it in your skin."

My fingers touch the base of my neck, and my nostrils flare in a frenzy. "You think this can contain me?"

"No, but I figured, now that you're awake, you're well enough to be transported back to your actual room." He flicks his fingers, and a bunch of guards steps forward to shove me onto the ground. They throw my arms on my back and snap two thick slabs of metal around my wrists and feet, locking me in place.

"Ready to go down, you filthy pig?" one of them spits as four of them haul me up from the floor.

They drag me through the hallway and down the

staircase into the main hall. But when I spot that damn door again, I panic.

"No, no, no!" I grunt.

I fight and fight as best I can, even with locked arms and legs, but every time I do, the button is pushed, and the pain makes all my muscles spasm intensely.

"Yes, Beast. Back where you belong," my owner growls as the door is opened, and the gateway to my own personal hell is right in front of me.

A deep, dark, damp cell.

Where every inch of light and hope are evaporated.

"Let me go!" I yell as they drag me back to the one place I vowed never to return.

My owner merely laughs as they shove me right back into the cell. "This is where you belong, just like the fucking Beast you are."

They spread my legs, pinning them to the wall, and fasten them with metal clasps to a new device drilled into the wall. Then they pin my arms spread-eagled to the wall with the same type of metal clasps, forcing me into an upright position, like a hanged man.

Both dead and alive.

"You promised me freedom!" I growl as my owner steps inside to gaze at me with disgust.

"And you promised to kill your target," he replies, grabbing my face and forcing me to look at him. "So I will keep you locked up in here as long as it fucking suits me, and you will fight for me when I tell you to. You think this is hell?" he asks through gritted teeth. "Imagine a pain a hundred times worse than death ... blasting you forever and ever." He tilts my head to gaze at whatever is buried in my neck. "Don't mistake my honor for kindness. When you forfeit your loyalty to me, you forfeit your soul."

When he turns to walk, I say, "What about the girl? Aurora?"

He pauses in his tracks, glaring at me over his shoulder. "What about her?"

"Did she escape?"

A vicious smile spreads on his face. "You really care more about her than your own life, don't you?"

I swallow, keeping my words to myself. He doesn't deserve them.

But judging from the annoyed look on his face, I definitely hit a chord.

He hasn't caught her.

Which means she's free.

And even though I'm in grave pain, it still brings an actual smile to my face.

The look on his face turns more monstrous than I could ever be. "I *will* find her, make no mistake. And when I do ..." he says, grinding his teeth. "I will make her my fuck doll and force you to watch."

Eight

Aurora

Present

I'm strapped to the van with actual metal cuffs now, and they sting against my skin. I try to ignore it and focus, but it's so damn hard. All I can think about is Beast.

He's alive.

He really is alive.

My heart flutters at the thought of seeing him again.

But then I remember Lex caught him, and my heart immediately sinks into my shoes.

What if they hurt him? Gave him so much pain his soul left his body?

What if he … gave up?

I swallow away the lump in my throat. I won't know until I see him for myself.

But what if Lex doesn't let me see him?

It would be just the kind of torturous thing he'd do just for fun.

"We're here," the driver says to the other guard, and the van stops.

After a few seconds, the door slides open, and I push myself off the floor to keep the guards from grabbing me but to no avail.

"No, don't touch me!" I scream as they grasp ahold of my legs and step inside.

"Shut up!"

SMACK!

The punch to my face is ruthless and instantly makes my cheeks red with pain.

I'm momentarily stunned by the harsh treatment.

Dave takes it as an opportunity to release my cuffs and unhook me from the van. The guards drag me out and violently shove my hands behind my back, tying them up again. "Don't fucking resist, or I'll smack you even harder next time," Dave says.

"You always hit defenseless girls?" I spit.

I don't know, but I've gotten so much more ready to throw back insults after what they put me through. I guess seeing death right in front of you and having your own father basically disown you as his daughter changes you.

"If you don't shut up, I'm going to put a dirty sock in your mouth," he growls, pointing at my face.

I imitate biting it off, and he immediately retracts his finger. "Goddamn filth."

I throw him a stink-eye, but another guard shoves me. "Walk. Now."

We go inside the mansion, the mere sight of the place making me cower in fear because I know all too well what happens inside. The door is already open, and a bunch of guards stare at me like I'm the cause of their misery.

"Where does Lex want me to take her?" one guard asks another.

"Lex is gone for the moment," another guard replies. "He left me in charge."

"Fine, where do you want her?"

"Down in the hole," the other guard replies.

My eyes widen, and I mutter, "The hole?"

Dave hits me on the head. "Don't fucking backtalk."

The guards shove me around and into the hallway, back to that same door I recognize all too well. But there's no sign of Lex anywhere, so I assume he's really gone.

Why?

I gasp.

Did they find my father?

In my mind, the image of my father with a bloodied face, lying on the floor, begging for his life while Lex holds a gun to his head keeps appearing.

But the wreck of emotions that would've washed over

me before are now dull. Muted.

I feel … very little.

Even though he used to be my papa. My father.

The man I used to look up to.

But now? There's nothing but regret.

I'm shoved down into the basement again, waltzing down the steps with a heavy heart.

Until I spot Beast.

My heart skips a beat a the sight of him hanging by four thick, metal clasps screwed into the wall, his head tilted forward, his body almost lifeless. I can barely contain my emotions.

The guard pushes me forward and then opens the cell door. "Get inside."

I do what he says without much resistance.

Not because I don't want to fight them, I do, even when I know I'll never win.

But because I want to see Beast myself, up close.

The guard quickly unlocks my hands and steps outside.

Tears well up in my eyes, and I don't even notice the guard shutting the door and walking up the stairs. All I can focus on is the fact that he's here in the flesh.

Even though he seems far from actually being alive.

"Beast?" I mutter, tears fluttering against my eyelashes.

His emerald eyes flash just the way they did the first time we met, when I was hiding underneath that piano, deathly afraid of what might happen to my father and me.

But now … now I'm simply relieved.

"Aurora …" he murmurs, raising his head to meet my gaze.

And I can no longer stop the tears from freely rolling down. "You … you're really alive."

Without thinking, I run to him and wrap my arms around his body to feel the warmth and comfort. Home.

He groans in agony, and I immediately pull back, gasping in shock that I actually did that. "I'm sorry. I don't want to hurt you."

"You *can't* … hurt me." His face is a mixture of calmness and pure and utter misery, as though he's trying to give me the best version of himself despite his pain.

A thick bandage is wrapped around his chest, stained with blood. All he's wearing is a pair of thin, linen lounge pants. His hands hang in the metal clasps, his body leaning forward as though his own body is weighing on him, gravity pulling him to the floor.

It looks so painful.

I jerk at the chains, but it's no use. They won't budge.

"I'm not dreaming," he mutters. It almost sounds like he can't believe it. "You're really here."

"Yes, I'm here," I reply, getting closer, but the second I think of touching his face, my hand freezes midair.

His eyes flash to my hand and then back to my face, the look in his eyes darkening. "You shouldn't be. I fought to keep you safe."

"I … I'm…" I blush and lower my eyes, stepping back. "They caught me when I went to look for you. I didn't want to end up in this cell again, either. I'm sor—"

"Don't," he interjects. "Don't say you're sorry. Do *not* be sorry." I'm hooked to his words and those soul-crushing eyes. "Did you fight for your freedom?"

I nod. More tears well up in my eyes. "But I should've stayed by your side, I should've helped, I—"

"You should've kept running," he interrupts.

Guilt fills my bones.

Maybe he's right.

But how could I stay away knowing he was there in that clinic, possibly dying of his wounds?

I had to know for sure. I had to see him for myself.

But now I've gotten myself in much bigger trouble.

"I needed to know if you were safe," I mutter. "I couldn't bear the thought of seeing you in that warehouse, dying a slow and painful death." I look at him and all the scars on his body.

"Maybe death would've been better," he murmurs. A few simple movements cause him so much pain he winces.

"What did they even do to you?" I mutter, looking at all the wounds on his body. There are more gashes than I remember there being.

"Too much," he growls.

"They even tied you up like you're some kind of monster," I mutter, abhorred at how they've chained him up to the wall.

"There's an implant too," he says, eyes rolling away. "In my neck."

I try to touch it, but the groan that follows makes me instantly remove my hand.

"It could kill me."

My eyes widen. "How?"

"If the voltage is upped to the max."

My jaw drops, but I swallow the gasp. "Who would do such a—"

"My owner …" he rasps, his eyes turning almost as black as the night with rage. "Lex."

It's the first time I've heard him say the man's actual name, but the fact that it's laced with such poison makes goose bumps scatter on my skin.

"How did he find you?" he asks.

I suck in a breath. "I heard about the clinic from someone, so I came to look …"

His lips part. "For me?"

I nod, and a gentle smile forms on his face, but it's immediately disrupted by a bloodied cough.

I rub my lips together and bring my hand to his chest, placing it on top of his heart. "What can I do?" I ask, feeling helpless.

He looks down at my fingers, and I immediately remove my hand, unsure if he even wants me to touch him.

"No," he murmurs, and he moves his hands, groaning in agony when the chains refuse to move with him. He's stuck to the wall while I'm right in front of him, his body straining with everything it has, trying to be free. To get … closer to me.

"Don't stop," he says.

I hold my breath and look him in the eyes, then slowly place my hand back where I'd put it. His body is hot and sweaty but still as rigid and toned as I remember, despite half of it being wrapped up in bandages.

All this time, I wondered how and why I felt such a strong connection to him, but I think I'm beginning to understand. His need for a better life clashing with my need to save my father blinded me from the truth.

"You freed my father …" I murmur, leaning in closer. "Even when it almost cost you your life. Why?"

He licks his lips, blood still clearly visible on his teeth. "Because you love him … and I'm in love with you."

I suck in a breath, but it still feels like I can't breathe.

He's … in love with me?

It's almost too impossible to comprehend. Because who in the world would want to love someone like me?

But maybe he fell for me before Lex took off my gloves.

I immediately become hyperaware of my ungloved hands, but his voice pulls me out of my thoughts.

"I wanted you to be free," he says. "More than I wanted to be freed."

I interrupt him with a kiss. I can't bear it any longer, this sense of gratitude. It's a desperate, overwhelming kiss that steals not only his breath but mine too. And I wish we could've met in a better life. Because this man … this man has stolen the one thing I thought I would never be able to give away: my heart.

"Thank you," I murmur again.

And I take the flower he gave me out of my pocket and stuff it back into his.

"Why?" he asks.

I smile. "Because I gave it to you once before … and I want you to keep holding on to hope."

I push myself up against him, not caring even a little bit about the consequences as he grows hard against the fabric of his thin pants. When I pull away for a second, he groans in agony, and I wonder if it's from the intense pain or from the frustration of not being able to touch me.

I don't want him to suffer, but there isn't much I can do. I can't free him from these chains.

But there is one thing I can do to ease his pain.

I press a kiss to his chin and on his neck, and judging from the strained puffs, he's dying for more. So I give him all I have to give, kissing his skin as I go lower and lower, pressing soft kisses to his chest and abs.

And when I lower myself in front of him, I look into his starry eyes, wondering if this is all it would take … to bring the beast to life.

Nine

BEAST

When she goes to her knees in front of me, my heart thumps and my cock swells with desire.

"What are you doing?" I say with a gruff voice.

She kisses the ridges of my thighs, slowly sliding down my lounge pants. "Making you forget. Making you feel better."

God, it feels like it's been ages since she last touched me there, yet the second her lips touch my skin, I remember all the reasons I wanted to keep her.

I was never this greedy, this overtaken by lust until I found her under that piano and took her with me.

I still feel guilty for that, and now she's down on her knees between my legs, kissing my pain away.

Fuck.

Nothing could excite me more than this.

But it's wrong, and she knows it. "You don't have to do this."

She pulls down the linen even farther until my hard cock is released and springs alive right up in her face. "But I want to."

When her lips wrap around my length, I lose all the words I had in my mind.

All that's left is the virulent lust thundering through my veins, reminding me of just how much I'm willing to sacrifice to feel this once again.

This. This is the reason I fought so hard. Why I couldn't do what my owner wanted me to.

Because this girl … this girl has mesmerized me to the point of losing myself.

And I'd happily die for her.

She brings her lip farther and farther down my shaft, and I groan with delight at the feel of her soft lips and wet tongue rolling around and around. It feels too good to be true, and it probably is, but if this is a dream spun by my feverish head, it's the best dream I've ever had. If I die, this is how I want it to happen; in full-blown ecstasy.

I never imagined being bound and getting my cock licked could ever be this … sexy.

I lick my lips from the growing arousal building in my

body as she works my dick, licking and sucking like her life depends on it. And I wish now more than ever that I was freed from these chains just so I could touch her face, feel those lips, push that head farther into my groin and come deep inside her.

I groan out loud from the sheer pleasure she's giving me, wondering what I did to deserve this. "Fuck," I mutter. "Deeper. Faster. Suck harder."

She does exactly what I demand from her, as though nothing makes her happier than pleasuring me, and the idea alone almost makes me want to jet out my cum right then and there.

She looks up at me with deep, dark eyes filled with such lust that I wonder if she missed me as much as I missed her.

"I …" My words are interrupted by a groan from deep within as she buries her face into my groin, struggling to keep the tears at bay.

I can't finish my sentence. I won't.

Because I refuse to put this on her, to make her feel guilty for running, to make her feel like she should've stayed by my side.

But my God, when she sucks me like that, it makes me want to break free and show her just how much I wished she could've been mine.

"I want you," I mutter, delirious from how good she's licking me. "So badly." The chains that hold me strain against my skin as I push my broken body to its limit.

She leans back, taking my cock out of her mouth while

gazing into my eyes. "Then take me. Make me yours." She pouts her lips. "Please."

Good God. Her voice. Those words.

Make me yours. Please.

A flurry of rage overcomes me, and I roar out loud as I pull as hard as I can with my left arm, pushing through the pain as it almost breaks my arm.

CLINK!

The screws break loose from the wall on one side, releasing my arm. And even though the metal is still attached to my wrist, my focus is solely on her.

And I bring my hand to her head, gently caressing her cheek for a second before I grab a fistful of her black hair and shove her mouth over my entire length and into my balls.

A massive moan rolls off my tongue as I bury myself inside her and come hard and fast, squirting my cum all over her throat.

She's gasping for air, but I don't relent, pulling out only to shove her right back on again, filling her to the brim.

When I'm finally satiated, my cum dribbles out of her mouth as she coughs and heaves.

But instead of letting it drop onto the floor, she catches it with her hands, brings it to her mouth, and licks it up.

All of it.

And fuck me, there is nothing that could make me want to break free from these chains faster than this woman when she's in heat.

"You undo me," I murmur, my heart and lungs still in overdrive. "If this is how I could die, I would lay down my life in a second."

She giggles and presses soft kisses all around my cock, as though she's dying for another taste, making me grow hard all over.

I wonder if she knows what she does to me.

If it's the reason she chose to do this.

I grab her face and tilt her chin to force her to look at me. "You wanted me to free myself."

When a blush creeps onto her cheeks, it's all I need to confirm my suspicions.

"I don't want to use you," she says. "But I want you to use me."

My cock hardens again just from those simple words.

Use her. Just like I wanted to back when she first came into my lair.

But this time ... It's not just to release the pent-up desire.

It's to break free of these chains, these walls that surround us.

"You've done it before," she mutters. "When I called your name, told you to fight ... you did. You made it happen." Her eyes tear up. "I don't want you to suffer, to be in pain. I want you to be as free as I was. Even if only for a little while."

My fist balls. "But it cost you *everything*."

Tears run down her cheeks, but I wipe them away with

my thumb. "I don't care what it costs me anymore," she says, and she steps away. "If I don't have the strength to free you …" she mutters as she tugs at the button of her black suit trousers and slowly pulls it down along with her panties until the naked, flushed skin of her pussy is exposed.

And my tongue darts out to wet my lips in response, eager, no, dying, for a taste.

But when I reach, the other metal clasps around my wrist and ankles hold me back.

"Then I will make you have the strength to free yourself," she adds.

Her fingers slide down her body, right between her crevice, the very place I would kill to touch right now. Just to ease the pain and claim what's mine.

But I can't.

I physically can't reach her, and she knows it drives me insane.

And when she starts playing with herself right in front of me, I turn back into that raging, animalistic beast I once was, groaning with frustration.

"I've never touched myself before," she murmurs, biting her lip, doubt lacing her eyes. "But I will … for you."

Oh God.

The mere sight of her standing there with quivering legs, begging for a release, makes me moan out loud.

"Don't do this to me, Aurora," I growl, panting with arousal as she splays her pussy and rolls her finger over her clit.

"I have to," she says, her fingers happily diving between her legs. "But I wish more than anything that you would do it."

Her cheeks grow redder and redder as she toys with herself, sinking deep into her own flesh.

My free hand instinctively reaches for her like a beggar tempted by food. I've experienced torture before, but no amount of pain, physical or mental, could come close to not being able to touch my woman.

"I know you can do it," she says, staring me in the eyes while playing with herself. "You've done it before."

I pull and tug at the chains as hard as I can, but to no avail. The nails are fiercely embedded into the wall, and my legs almost break from the pressure alone.

"God, I feel so dirty," she murmurs. "I wasn't ever allowed to do this. But it feels … so … good." Her mouth forms an o-shape when she sticks a finger inside.

I'm salivating at the mouth, and it even drips down the sides of my lips and onto the concrete floor. That's how frantic I am to have a single touch or lick. And my cock is already fully erect again, just from the mere idea of claiming her.

But I fucking can't, and it's destroying me.

"You're killing me," I say through gritted teeth. "I want it. I want *you* … so badly."

She tilts her head, exposing her neckline, running her fingers down her chest, her nipples, and it makes me swallow with heat.

"Then take what's yours," she murmurs.

That's it.

I breathe out loud as all my muscles begin to tense and twitch. "You don't know what you're unleashing," I hiss.

She pushes up and down into her pussy and pulls out her fingers to show me the wetness sticking between. "Then show me what you're willing to do, or I'll do it myself."

Enough.

Howling like an animal, I tear away at my own muscles to rip these metal clasps around my legs to shreds, just like I did to the metal around my neck when she begged me to fight. And now she's begging me to make her mine, so I will.

When my feet finally rest on the ground, free of the chains that kept me bound to these walls, I tug at the final chain keeping me in place.

She stops moving her fingers entirely, and her chest rises and falls quickly when I take a heavy step forward. And another one. One more, and I'm right in front of her petite frame, towering over her like a mountain, ready to crush whatever is in its path.

There is only one thing in this entire world that I want more than freedom, more than life itself.

Her.

My hand snakes around her throat, and she gasps for air as I twist her around and push her against the wall. My free hand slides down across her shirt, her tits and peaked nipples, across her belly, and between her legs.

"This," I groan, pushing my middle finger onto her clit,

"is *mine*."

She mewls with delight when I begin rolling my fingers around between her thighs, spreading her wetness before I dive inside. Her lips form another o-shape, and I capture her gasp with an all-consuming kiss, stealing her breath away.

Everything that is her belongs to me. She always was, from the moment we first met until now. Her kisses, her touches, her orgasms, her moans, even her very fucking breaths.

And I need every droplet of wetness too.

So I lean in and listen to her ragged breaths getting increasingly unhinged as I slowly drive her insane with lust, flicking my fingers back and forth. And with a dirty smile, my tongue dips out to drag a line from her ear to her neck, tasting the sweet, salty mix of sweat and desire.

"You make this hell taste like heaven," I groan.

She moans when I shove another finger inside. "Oh God."

"Yes, Aurora, I am your fucking god."

Her eyes are transfixed on mine as I coax out her hunger for more. And her hips begin to gyrate against my hand.

"Is this what you wanted?" I ask.

She nods, barely able to reply through the heady moans.

"You taunted me," I whisper into her ear, my fingers tightening around her neck so I can feel her pulse quickening with every breath. "Now give me what I'm owed."

"Yes," she mewls, her eyes almost rolling into the back

of her head.

"That's it. Show me what I live for, what I'd die for," I groan as she falls apart at the seam.

Her pussy contracts around my fingers, spreading delicious juices as her legs begin to buck. She can barely stay standing, but I keep her pinned against the wall, thrusting in and out, flicking her clit like no tomorrow to coax out another orgasm.

The face she gives me is one of pure ecstasy, and if I could see this face for all eternity in death, I'd end my life right this very second. That's how gorgeous she looks when she gives me everything she has to give. Again, and again, and again, until all that's left of her is a whimpering, shaking, wet mess.

When I finally release her from my grip, she sinks to the floor like a used rag doll, breathing irregularly as though her heart can barely keep up with the orgasmic waves flooding her body.

And I stroke my cock with fervor, not giving a shit that she's out of energy to do anything about it.

She taunted the beast, and now she'll have him, raging hard-on and all.

"You belong to me," I groan, flicking my hand back and forth across the tip of my length. "And every single one of your orgasms is *mine*."

I roar out loud and thrust in my own hand, releasing myself, jetting my cum all over her body beneath me. I jerk off a few more times until I've finally let go of all that pent-up anger and lust and blow out a few heavy breaths.

Suddenly, the door at the top of the stairs opens, and a guard waltzes down. Aurora quickly raises her pants back up over her waist before anyone sees. I do the same with my linen pants, ensuring the flower isn't damaged.

"Hey, you! What's that ruck—Fuck." The guard stops and stares at us halfway down the steps, his gaze slowly focusing on Aurora in shock. "Who the fuck put you in here!?"

He immediately approaches the cell and grabs his walkie-talkie. "We got a problem in the cell. Need some backup. I don't know how, but he's out of the chains."

I march toward him and slam my fists through the bars, narrowly missing his face by a hair. He quickly sidesteps out of my reach.

"You motherfuc—"

He pulls out a tiny box with a few buttons on it, the same one my owner used to keep, and presses it.

The pain is instant, intense, but above all, cruel.

I sink to my knees, roaring in pain.

"No! Don't hurt him!" Aurora yells behind me, but I can barely hear her voice through the visceral spasm twisting my body.

This new device is ten times worse than the collar ever was.

Fuck.

How am I going to survive this agony?

"Get her out of there!" the guard yells as some of his

fellow guardsmen come downstairs.

"What? No," Aurora yelps as the men open the door and step inside with a bunch of them.

And all I can do is watch helplessly as they drag her out of the cell and up the stairs.

"Beast!" she calls, her voice going through marrow and bone.

"Aurora!" I yell back. But my body refuses to listen with this extreme zapping forcing my limbs into odd shapes.

"If you fucking touch her, I swear …" I say through gritted teeth, barely able to speak.

The guard in front of me laughs as his buddies close the cell again. "You'll what? Drool a little?" He sniggers and turns around.

The electrical current finally relents when he's at the top of the stairs.

I breathe in deep, forcing the pain to leave my body as I get up to stand. My muscles quake with my every move, but I still approach the bars and yell, "I WILL KILL YOU ALL!"

Ten

Aurora

"No, take me back!" I yelp as they drag me through the hallway and into the living room area, where I come face-to-face with Lex himself.

The mere sight of his deathly gaze has me boiling with rage.

"Well, I've never heard anyone beg so loudly to be put back into a dark hole again." He laughs out loud. "You're really smitten with him, aren't you?"

He laughs so hard that he coughs, and he pulls out a napkin from his pocket and wipes his mouth. There's blood.

But I don't care if he's hurt or not. He hurt Beast and me. This man deserves zero compassion.

"You shot him!" I yell in anger. "How dare you? He did the right thing, and you repaid him by almost killing him."

"*Almost* being the keyword here." He winks. "And what's right is subjective."

"That's bullshit, and you know it," I retort.

"He let you run, and what was the reward?" he muses. "His own near-death and more pain." Lex shakes his head. "All thanks to you."

He flicks his fingers, and the guards put me on a couch near the fireplace.

"Who put her in that cell?" he asks one of his guards.

"Uh …" the man stutters.

"Find out. Punish them with the whip," Lex says, and the guards immediately walk off, talking amongst themselves.

Two guards remain in the room to guard the place while Lex sits down on the seat opposite me. He grabs a cigar from a box off the table and sticks it in his mouth, then fishes a lighter from his pocket to fire it up, all while keeping his gaze fixed on me.

But I'm not intimidated easily by him anymore.

"Let. Me. Go," I hiss, clutching the couch's armrest.

He snorts. "Give me one good reason."

"Why do you even need me in the first place?" I ask.

"You were with your father when you ran," he says, taking another drag of his cigar, blowing out the smoke in my direction. "You know where he is."

"You think I'd tell you where he is?" I scoff.

He raises a brow. "He hurt you, didn't he?"

Sweat drops roll down my back. "You did too."

"It must be so tough living in a world where even your own family doesn't want you," he says, steamrolling over me and my emotions. "Where your own father calls you a monster."

"Don't," I say, tears welling up in my eyes.

"Or what?" He blows out more smoke after taking another drag. "You think you have any power in this world?" He gets up from his seat, towering over me. "You live only because I let you live."

"I'm alive thanks to Beast and no one else," I say through gritted teeth, pushing back the tears.

"And that mistake will cost him dearly," he growls back.

My eyes widen. "You wouldn't—"

"Kill him?" His nostrils flare, and he steps forward and violently grabs me by the hair, forcing me to look at him. "He is my hound. My killer. And you stole him from me."

"He *chose* me instead of you," I say.

"Because of you flaunting that pussy all over him," he spits, his face turning red. "Just like you did a minute ago when my guards foolishly put you in that same cell again."

He chucks me back into the couch, towering over me like he wants to strike me. "But I'm glad you came to that clinic … because now I can make you pay."

He flicks his fingers, and the two guards at the door leave the room.

"What are you going to do?" I mutter, trying to lean

away, but he's right in front of me, preventing me from running.

"What I should have done the first time he brought you back," he growls, tilting his head with a menacing look. "What I've wanted to do ever since you wore that pretty dress."

My eyes widen as he lowers his hands to his pants and pulls the button.

Oh God. This can't be happening. Not again.

"Now … are you going to tell me where your father is?" he muses, zipping down. "Or do you want me to *make* you?"

I spit in his face.

He turns and wipes it off.

And I immediately regret it when his eyes land on me.

Suddenly, the doors open again, and in step those same guards … dragging Beast along with them. He's in chains, both wrists and ankles, and he looks like he's in so much pain that it brings tears to my eyes. They must've zapped him so hard he lost consciousness.

When he finally raises his head and meets my gaze, I swallow, barely able to mutter the word. "Beast."

His eyes fall back into his head as they drag him to a chair and position it right in front of the couch, strapping him to it with the chains.

Lex pulls out a knife and snarls at me, "Get up."

I do what he asks. Within seconds, he cuts through the fabric of my shirt, shredding it to pieces, and it all falls to the floor. Teardrops roll down my cheeks as he removes it all, and I'm left half-naked. But even that isn't enough. He slashes at the fabric of my trousers until those are completely destroyed too, and all that's left are my panties … which he cuts away too.

I cross my hands over my body, attempting to hide, but Lex wags a finger back and forth.

"Ah-ah. Let's see what he likes so much about you that he was willing to throw it all away," Lex says, and he points the knife at my chest until I remove my hands.

All my private parts are on display as if it doesn't even matter.

Even the guards are still here, gaping at me, grinning like savages.

And it makes me feel so tiny I can't even breathe.

"Now is when the good part starts," Lex says, lifting my chin. "My fucking hound gets to watch me fuck his little toy as payback."

Panic floods my veins, but Lex pushes the knife to my throat when I attempt to move.

"Now open your pretty little mouth, girl …" he says, zipping down.

"NO!" Beast roars from his seat.

Everyone watches Beast as he raises his head, grinding his teeth so hard they might break. "Touch her, and you die."

Lex begins to laugh. "I'm already dying. But go ahead and try."

Beast growls in pain as he tears away at the chains by

simply flexing his muscles.

The guards behind him try to hold him back but to no avail. He chucks them aside with ease, throwing the chair along with it, crushing one of them.

"LEAVE. HER. ALONE!" His roars sound like an animal as he breaks the last piece of metal holding him back.

Lex merely smirks and pulls the same tiny box from his pocket, pressing the button.

Beast instantly collapses onto the wooden floor, writhing in pain.

"Please, stop," I beg. "Don't do this to him, please! I'll do what you want."

"No, girl. This dog needs to learn his place first," Lex growls, taking pleasure in seeing Beast writhe in pain.

He's beyond cruel, and I don't know what else to do.

Without thinking, I lunge forward and press the other button, releasing Beast from his agony.

"You bitch, let go!" Lex smacks me hard.

Stars fill my eyes as I flop back onto the couch.

Beast's howl fills the room as he charges at Lex. "Shoot him!"

BANG! BANG!

Gunshots fill the room.

Everything happens too fast for me to register.

Beast suddenly scoops me off the couch and runs toward the only exit in the room that's unguarded; the window.

"No, you fucking won't!" Lex growls, and I can feel him

press the button because the electrical current also goes through me.

The pain is so intense I nearly vomit, and Beast almost drops me. Near the floor, he groans in pain, suffering but still refusing to let go. Instead of giving up, he pushes himself up, despite the electricity roasting him alive. And with every last inch of strength he has, he storms at the window with me in his arms, turning around just in time so he can smash it with his back.

CRASH!

The sound of glass fragments falling to the floor fills my ears as we burst through the window and into a bush.

The electrical current stops immediately, but I can barely stand from the pain, let alone look around.

Arms wrap around my naked waist and pull me out of the bush, but I can only focus on those mesmerizing emerald eyes. The eyes of a beast carrying me away from the real monsters.

Eleven

BEAST

I bolt to the nearest car with Aurora in my arms and open the door by kicking it with pure force. The key is still inside the ignition. Those fuckers didn't even bother locking it after bringing her back to the mansion. They were far too busy pleasing their fucking boss to even notice they screwed up.

BANG!

Aurora shrieks and ducks for cover inside the car.

I jump in behind her, crawling over her to the driver's seat.

No time to waste. They're shooting at us from the window.

"Don't let them escape!" Lex roars across the grounds.

But I've already started up the engine and smashed the pedal. The tires screech as I turn the wheel and drive across the pavement, skidding on the road. I pay no attention to how fast I'm going. It's not fast enough.

"Oh, God, oh God!" Aurora panics beside me, clutching her naked body like it's her last lifeline.

I'm driving like the devil is coming after us. Because when I look through the rearview mirror, I can clearly see five or more guards running after us with guns at the ready.

BANG!

Another shot enters the vehicle from behind, and I steer as fast as I can.

"Hold on!" I yell as we approach the gate.

"What are you going to do? No, you can't—" Her words are interrupted by her own shriek as I drive straight through the barrier.

The front of the car takes the biggest hit as the light is smashed to bits. But we made it through.

I veer onto the main road and keep driving as fast as possible, ignoring the speed limit. Cars next to me and behind me beep loudly when I pass them and cut them off, but I don't give a shit.

"Oh my God, Beast," Aurora says, anxiety lacing her voice. "You're bleeding!"

I follow her eyes down to a wound in my abdomen oozing blood. A bullet must've grazed me.

Fuck. I don't have time for this. "Not now."

Right now, we have to get as far away from those fuckers as possible.

Because if they manage to catch up … it will be literal hell waiting for us both.

I ignore the pain and drive even faster. If we want to survive, I have to give it my all.

Aurora holds on to her tits and the door as if she's scared she'll fall out and simultaneously flash someone. But right now, that's the least of our problems.

Behind us are two other black cars with blacked-out windows, and I definitely recognize them.

"They're on our tail," I say.

"Oh no," she mutters, peering out the back window. "Drive faster!"

"I'm trying," I say, but someone in front of me won't let me pass.

I hit the brakes only to veer sideways and pass them when they aren't looking, stomping the gas and sticking up my middle finger when they look. Aurora is mortified when they see her nude body, and she quickly dives for cover on the floorboard.

"Stay there," I say. "Better for when they shoot."

"*When* they shoot?" She gasps. "It's broad daylight!"

"That won't stop him," I reply, hitting sixth gear and racing off. "We need more traffic. Civilians are the only thing getting in their way."

I veer left and right, hopping from lane to lane, switching up the tempo to get between all the cars. When I look to my left, I spot something that could be of use: A very old car parked on someone's driveway, not too far from this road.

I get off the highway as quickly as possible and turn around multiple times toward a road marked as a dead-end.

I park there, and fish a small gun from the overhead bin, then hop out.

"What are you doing?" Aurora hisses at me from the floorboard.

"Getting a new car," I growl back and walk to the door.

I press the doorbell a couple of times until someone finally opens up and shrieks at the sight of my half-naked body.

"Jezus Christus!" a woman yells incensed, and she almost shuts the door again, but I put a foot between. "Wat wil je? Waarom ben je halfnaakt?!"

I can understand some Dutch, but not much. Something about me being half-naked, that's for sure.

I firmly grab ahold of the door so she can't close it. "Give me your car keys."

"No, why the fuck would I?"

When I raise the gun, she yelps and puts her hand in the air. "Okay, okay, don't shoot!"

She walks back slowly.

"Give me the keys. Now."

She fishes behind the staircase in some kind of locker and throws it at me. I barely manage to catch it. "Take it. Take anything. I don't care. Just don't kill me, please."

"Your phone," I say, holding out my hand.

She sighs out loud and chucks it my way. "Fine. Take it and leave."

"Clothes," I bark.

"What?" she stammers.

"Your clothes!"

"Okay, okay," she mutters, taking off her shoes and socks and throwing them my way. Next are her pink, fluffy sweater and jeans. The only thing she leaves on are her panties, but I won't need those.

I look over my shoulder to make sure Aurora is still safe in the car.

"There, you have my clothes. Now get out," the woman says. "Leave!"

I wasn't planning on staying longer than needed anyway. I know she'll call the police the second I leave the premise, but I don't care. They'll never find Aurora or me.

Where we're going, no one even knows we'll exist.

I walk toward our car and throw the woman's clothes to Aurora. "Put these on." Then I march to the woman's car to unlock it.

"What's going on? How did you get these?" Aurora asks as she puts on the pink sweater.

"Don't ask questions you don't wanna know," I say, shoving the gun into the overhead bin of the new car. "Now c'mon."

She quickly puts on her new jeans, socks, and shoes and hops out only to jump right back into the passenger's seat of our new one.

"We can't just take it," she mutters as I turn on the engine.

"Yes, we can, and we will," I growl, putting it in reverse and racing off.

The woman stares at us through her window with another phone next to her ear.

Aurora's face goes white.

"Don't worry about her," I say. "She'll never see us again."

She suddenly turns to look at me. "We have to bring the car back."

"What?" I frown. "No way. That's too dangerous."

"When we're no longer being hunted," she adds. "When everything is … safe."

That last word sounded heavy.

Too heavy.

But I don't know what safe is.

I've never felt it.

"Someday," she says, a gentle smile forming. "We will."

I don't know if it's possible, but if it makes her feel better to dream about it, I won't stop her.

Still, there's no time to think about this now. Lex's men are still on our tail.

I swiftly make a U-turn with the car and drive onto the road. I try to blend in with the rest of the traffic without speeding too much.

When I look through the mirror, the blacked-out cars

appear again.

"Oh God, they're here," she says, panicking. "But how? They don't know we have this car."

I grab her hand and squeeze it tight. "Focus on me."

She nods, shivering in place.

"Hide," I say, and she immediately slips off the seat to the floorboard again.

Sweat drops trickle down my forehead as the cars behind us speed up.

But they don't know it's us yet. They couldn't possibly know.

But what if they look inside?

I swiftly reach into the bin and search for anything I can find. A thick piece of fabric, a scarf. Perfect.

I take my hands off the wheel for a second to quickly wrap it around my head and secure it tight. I look ridiculous, but it might camouflage me enough to hide my face while I drive.

The cars are approaching fast.

I make a turn to the right.

My muscles tighten as I anxiously wait to see.

But they don't follow.

Instead, they drive off to the main road, swerving left and right, still looking for that one car that's not there anymore.

Excitement flows through my veins.

"They didn't see us?" she mutters.

I shake my head. "They'll probably find the car soon." A

broad smile forms on my face. "But not before we're long gone."

And I hit the gas and race off.

When we're finally somewhere safe, I park the car in a free parking lot and take some time to breathe. Aurora finally gets the courage to sit back on her seat again instead of hiding underneath the headboard.

"Are we … safe?" she asks.

"They're not following us," I reply.

"But safety is another thing," she murmurs. "We'd need a house for that. Or at least somewhere to stay. And I'm definitely not going back to that hotel my father was staying at."

She gasps in shock, grasping my arm. "My father! He's still in there. What if they go after him?"

"Not your problem anymore," I reply.

Her face darkens. "But …"

My hand instinctively rises to caress her cheek. I don't like seeing her worry. Especially not about someone who doesn't even care about her. "He can handle himself."

She swallows. "But where do we go now?"

I take in a deep breath. "I don't know."

Her eyes suddenly flicker as though a light bulb went on in her brain. "I know one more secret hideout my father never told anyone about. It wasn't even in his documents."

My eyes narrow. Anything that involves her father feels like a bad idea. "Are you sure that's safe?"

"Lex can't know about it," she replies. "My father would

never tell anyone about his precious vacation home. There's nothing of value to steal."

She reaches in the overhead bin and fishes out the phone I stuffed in there. She opens it up and checks some app for locations. "Here." She points at an area on the map not too far from where we're at. "It's a small house near the beach."

"Are you sure?" I ask. I don't trust any of this, but when she nods and smiles at me with a cutesy face, I can't help myself. "Okay." I put the car in reverse. "You trusted me. So now I'll trust you."

***

When we finally arrive at the place she marked, I'm too flabbergasted to even properly check my surroundings, in case anyone followed us. Because in front of us is a very tiny house near the sea. And it's beautiful. Idyllic, even.

Unlike anything I'd ever associate with her father.

"My mother bought this when they were younger," Aurora says, and she shuts the car door.

Well, that explains it.

"You like it?" she muses as we walk toward the house.

"Sure," I reply.

She frowns. "You're not the least bit excited, are you?"

I don't know what she wants from me, so I opt not to say anything at all as we make our way to the front door.

"You don't talk much, do you?" she says.

My nostrils flare. "Talking only got me into more pain."

She makes a face. "I'm sorry."

"Don't be," I say. "It's not your fault."

"I'm just glad we're out of there," she says. "And hopefully in one piece." She giggles in an awkward manner, almost like she doesn't know how to act around me now that we're not inside that cage anymore.

She jumps up to a ledge above the door and fishes a key from there. "Yes! It's still here!"

Doesn't seem that safe to me to keep keys there. Then again, this is just the kind of thing I'd expect from the likes of Blom.

"My mother's idea," Aurora muses. "In case I'd ever need a safe space."

"Hmm … She could see into the future?" I say as Aurora opens the door.

"No, but she definitely knew what my father's job was. And from what I got told by our staff … she wanted to protect me from it, even before I was born." The last bit of her sentence comes out in a sigh as though she's still mourning her mother's loss.

I used to be like that too before the streets hardened me. Before I was snatched and shown that emotions only get you killed.

The door closes behind me, and I look around. Aurora checks out some of the furniture like she's physically touching up on memories.

Right next to me is a door that leads into what appears

to be the only bathroom. The kitchen and living room are open to each other, and in the back is an open door with a smaller room with a queen-sized bed.

"It's not amazing, but …"

"It's perfect."

Twelve

Aurora

I turn to look at him. "You think so?"

He nods. "It's more than I ever had."

I begin to blush, and I tuck a strand of hair behind my ear to try to hide it, but obviously, it fails because his eyes are definitely flicking back and forth across my face. "Oh, I never thought about it like that. I'm sorry, it was inconsiderate of me. I—"

He plants a finger on my lips, silencing me. "Stop apologizing. You've done more than enough of that."

I blush and avert my eyes, but then I notice the bleeding wound on his stomach. Shit, I completely forgot about that.

"Right, we have to find some supplies." I run to the bathroom and search the cabinets until I find a box.

"What supplies?" he asks from the living room.

I return with the box and open it up, pulling out some alcohol, a cotton pad, some sterile gauze, and tape. I place it on the kitchen counter and sit down on one of the stools, then pat my hand on the other. "Sit."

He ogles me for a moment like he's questioning my intentions.

"C'mon, let me help you," I say.

He sighs and then begins to walk toward me, each step like a stomp on the floor. And the sound still manages to make me gulp.

He's just so … huge.

Even when he sits on the stool in front of me, his muscles still look like they're about to bulge out of those flimsy linen pants.

My cheeks begin to flush again, but I push the raunchy thoughts away and focus on the task at hand. His wound looks gnarly and in need of a cleaning.

"Can you bend sideways? Just a little bit," I ask.

He does what I ask without complaining, but when I place a cotton pad with alcohol on his side, he hisses.

"Sorry, I know it stings," I say. "But it seems like it's only a graze. I don't see a bullet."

"I've felt worse," he says, laughing, then wincing.

And I can't help but wonder if he means that newly installed device.

Not that it matters. We're out of Lex's claws now.

There's no way he can hurt Beast or me from this distance. I'm sure that device won't work from this far away.

Which means … he should definitely get even farther away.

I sigh as I finish up and put some tape over the gauze, sealing the wound. "All done."

"Thanks," he says as I put the supplies away.

He gets off the seat and walks to the window to check the neighborhood. "It doesn't look like anyone's followed us here."

"I hope not," I respond, clearing my throat.

He's still staring out the window, hands splayed on the glass like he's looking out into a world he's yet to discover. And it makes me feel like I'm holding him back.

"You're free to go wherever you want now," I say.

"What?" He turns to me as his eyes darken. "What do you mean?"

I don't know what to say. "I just … don't want you to think you have to stay here."

"Why wouldn't I stay?" he asks, approaching me.

"Well, you're free now. You can go anywhere you like."

He walks closer, invading my space in a way that feels intimate. Exciting.

"I don't *want* to leave."

He pauses. The air is thick with tension.

Why wouldn't he want to leave?
He has the world at his feet.

All the freedom he could ever want.

"I don't want to leave *you*."

That one added word.

God.

I don't even know what to say.

"You've done more for me than anyone ever has," he says, taking my breath away.

But I'm just little me. I didn't do anything except try to save my papa, but it almost cost him his life.

"I almost got you killed. Twice," I mutter, tears welling up in my eyes at the thought.

He grabs my face, clutching me tight. "I'm alive, thanks to you."

I shake my head. That doesn't make any sense. I'm the reason he wasn't freed to begin with. The reason he chose to defy his owner.

But his fingers squeeze my cheeks, refusing to let me look anywhere other than into his mesmerizing green eyes.

"When I was brought back to that cell, I wanted to die. Until you gave me back the will to live."

I gasp as he leans in and presses a gentle but seductive kiss on my lips that pushes all my buttons and makes my heart flutter.

When his lips briefly pull away from mine, he whispers, "Thank you."

I shake my head even though our lips are still touching. "Don't thank me."

"Don't tell me what I can't do," he rebukes, pulling

away slowly.

He fishes into his pocket and takes out the flower I once gave him, still beautiful, even though it's dried up. "*This … this is what kept me going all these years.*"

I suck in a breath, the sight of that flower still making me feel like I'm spinning.

It's still so hard to believe I'm looking at the same boy I once found hiding in the tub. "You're really him…" I mutter. Now he's all grown up and … handsome.

Not at all the way I saw him when he first marched into my home like a lumbering, menacing giant determined to kill everything in sight.

"Is that why you couldn't kill me when you came for my father?" I ask.

I hadn't dared to ask the question before, but now that we're here, in a safe space, I have to know the truth.

He nods and grabs my face. "When I looked into your eyes, I recognized you."

I gulp, my heart skipping a beat.

"I knew it was you when I saw that same look. That look you gave me …" he murmurs, softly caressing my cheek. "But I also knew my owne—Lex"—he pauses, like it costs him a great deal to say Lex's name—"was watching through the camera in my collar. I couldn't risk him finding out."

No wonder he didn't want me to touch him at the hotel, despite him being interested in me soon after I was forced into his cell.

I grab his hand holding the flower and look at it. "I can't believe you kept it … all those years," I mutter. "How?"

His eyes lower as he dives into his memories. "I kept it safe in my pocket, even when the snatchers stole me. I hid it in the walls or underneath the floorboards, any place I could find." He holds it up in front of his face like it's the most precious jewel he's ever seen. "And when life got too rough, I'd take it out and just stare. For a moment. That's it."

Tears well up in my eyes, but when one rolls down, he lifts his thumb to my face and wipes it off.

"Don't cry," he says as he lowers the flower again.

I don't know what to say.

No words could ever carry the weight of my emotions or his.

So when he leans in to peck me on the lips, I give in completely.

"I'm here now," he murmurs against my lips. "I've found you, and you belong with me."

He keeps kissing me even though he's still holding that flower, and I am terrified of ruining it, of destroying the only thing that's kept him going for all these years.

But I don't want him to stop kissing me, either.

His kisses are like oxygen. I need them to survive.

But he still pulls away, even when I struggle desperately to hold his mouth with mine.

Suddenly, he swoops me up into his arms, and I shriek from the surprise. "What are you doing?"

"Giving you what you deserve …" he replies, making

me feel tingly in all the right places.

When did I begin to feel so much for a beast like him?

Was it before or after he first touched me? Kissed me? Made sure I knew I was his?

Days and nights blurred into one in that dark, damp cell, and my body adjusted, but my mind … my mind is still playing catch-up.

He carries me into the bedroom and heads straight for the bath, where he puts me down and starts tearing off my clothes. The shirt first, then my pants, as well as my socks and shoes. Not that they were mine, to begin with, but still … it makes me self-conscious because I'm naked once again.

I protect myself with my arms, despite knowing my hands are visible to him. But he doesn't seem to pay even the slightest attention to them as he throws my clothes in a corner and turns on the faucet.

The warm running water feels like bliss compared to the lukewarm shower we had back in the cell. But it feels wrong to be the only one to enjoy these simple things.

"You deserve a shower too," I mutter, not knowing what else to say.

He plants a finger on my lips and opens the faucet even further until the water starts gushing out. "My woman *always* comes first."

His woman?

Why does that make me feel so warm and fuzzy inside?

I huddle into the warm blanket of the water, trying to

hide my blush beneath the bubbles he poured in. It all smells so lovely, and it's a nice way to rinse off the nastiness from being in that mansion.

There was only ever one highlight, and it was always when he came to my rescue.

When he spread his arms and shielded me from their evil.

And I'm so grateful for everything he's done for me, for us … fighting his way through the pain to get us to safety … that I feel like he deserves this more than I do.

***

BEAST

I grab a bottle of soap from the counter near the bath and lather it with my hands before I grab her foot and lift it.

"Whoa—"

She swallows her squeal as I begin to massage her foot. I rub the soap gently across her legs, putting effort into every inch of her skin. Because every inch of her deserves to be treated with the utmost care.

To me … she is a goddess to worship.

As delicate as the flower she once offered me, the flower I once worshipped the same way.

She looks up at me from her warm bath like a doe

staring into the headlights.

It's the same look she gave me when I was strung up on the wall after letting her escape.

Caused by a mind overtaken by guilt.

I don't wait one second before I lean in, grab her face, and press a ravenous kiss on her pouty lips.

I don't need to hear the words to know what she's thinking or feeling inside that shattered heart of hers.

She's convinced herself that she doesn't deserve even a speck of kindness, even when she's the complete embodiment.

But I will make her see.

I will make her believe.

I don't stop kissing her, not even as she gasps for air. My lips are greedy and overbearing as I kiss her relentlessly.

My cock grows hard under these linen pants, but I will it to go down as I shower her in all the kisses she needs to make this ache go away.

And when I've finally been able to coax out her tongue, I step into the tub with her.

Her eyes widen in shock, and she pulls away, clutching her body. "What are you doing?"

I grab her legs and put them beside me while I sit down in the water on my knees. There's barely enough room for me, let alone the two of us, but I make it work by cupping her ass and lifting it.

She splashes around like a fish on dry land, redness flushing her skin as I lift her body to my face.

"Beast, I—"

While looking up into her eyes with possessive greed, I plant my lips against her inner thighs and growl, "Let me give you what you need …" I groan, sliding my lips down to her pussy. "What you deserve."

When I press my mouth onto her pussy she stops protesting, despite her raised finger. And it brings a smile to my face.

I lap her up with glee, not giving a shit that my linen pants are soaking wet or that my giant boner strains the fabric. All I care about is pleasuring this woman, my woman.

I need her to feel good and know exactly how to do it.

So I keep licking and circling her clit with my tongue, providing ample pressure. Her body begins to move along to my rhythm, her thighs swaying in my hands, her ass tightening with every stroke I apply.

Her taste is so good that it makes my mouth water as I dive in deep. My tongue thrusts into her pussy, and her moans are like music to my ears. I probe her pussy and suck on her clit until it's swollen and throbbing with need. And I love how I can see her slowly fall apart just from my tongue.

Goose bumps erupt on her body as I alternate licks with plunges and sucks, and her pussy begins to get soaking wet. Not from the water but from her own desires, breaking free of their constraint.

All this time, she kept her own needs on a leash, always thinking about someone else first, always putting other people's needs before hers.

No more.

"Beast, stop, I—"

"No," I groan into her pussy, cupping her ass to shove my face further into her. "I want you to come all over my mouth."

"What?" She gasps, her jaw dropping.

"You heard me," I say between the licks. "Drown me with your wetness."

She mewls when I thrust my tongue inside again, wetness pouring out.

"Rub your clit along my tongue," I say, coaxing her to bring out her impure side.

"But that's so wrong," she mutters, biting her lip as she struggles to keep the orgasm at bay.

"It's only wrong because you tell yourself it is. Because you've been led to believe you don't deserve all the raunchy, delicious parts of your own body." I circle her clit, which is thumping with need. "But I'm here to claim it all, and I won't stop until you give me *everything*."

"Fuck …" she says through gritted teeth.

She doesn't swear often, so I know I'm hitting the right spot.

"That's it, Aurora. Take what you need from me. Just like I took from you what I needed in that cell," I say.

Finally, she starts gyrating her hips against my mouth, and fuck me, it's the best feeling ever.

"Yes, rub your pussy all over my mouth," I groan, lapping her up like we'll die here in this tub. And even if we did, I'd have no regrets.

And when she finally falls apart against my tongue, I keep circling around and thrusting into her pussy until I've lapped up all of her wetness.

My cock is so damn hard it almost hurts, but I don't even care. All I want to do is make her feel good.

So I lower her into the tub again and lick my lips, not wasting a drop of any of that goodness. I turn off the faucet as the bath is filled up completely. But she suddenly crawls toward me, eyes filled with ravenous hunger.

Thrilling.

She pushes herself onto my lap and slides her hand down my chest and abs until she reaches the rim of my pants. I suck in a breath when she pushes it down, leans in, and whispers into my ear, "Please … I need to feel you inside me."

Fuck. Me.

How could I ever resist that kind of begging?

Thirteen

Aurora

Without thinking, I pull his cock out of his pants.

It bobs up and down, hard as a rock, thick and throbbing with pre-cum.

And it still makes me gulp.

Not just from the sheer size but from the idea that he could get this hard ... because of me.

Because his tongue was on my clit. Because I came from his mouth.

It feels so shameful yet liberating at the same time.

He made me feel so good, even when it felt so wrong, and I want to give that back to him. I know he needs it. His cock has been practically bursting out of his pants ever since we came to this beach house, and we finally had some time to breathe. To talk. To kiss.

And I don't want to stop.

If I could, I would continue forever, just to avoid having to think another day.

So I wrap my arms around his neck and press my lips to his.

He tastes of me, and it's sexy. I kiss him like he kissed me, still drunk on lust from that amazing orgasm he just gave me.

And I spread my legs and sink down onto his cock without saying a word.

His tongue instantly darts out and parts my lips forcefully, thrusting in to claim mine as I push myself down over his base. His rigid shaft pulsates inside me, and it's the best feeling in the world.

I tear my lips away for a moment to ask, "Is this what you want?"

His hands are on my thighs, nails digging into my skin. "I *need* it."

It's all I need to give him my body. I want to make him feel good, just like he made me feel good. And if that's a crime, so be it.

I'm not married, and I doubt I ever will be, but at least I've made the one man who deserves it happy.

The ridges on his brows slowly lower as his face begins to scrunch up, ready for the inevitable explosion of pleasure. And I witness it all right from his very lap, every second even more amazing than the one before. This beautiful broken man is falling apart from what I'm doing, and it feels so damn empowering that I can't get enough.

Even though I know I shouldn't be doing this, even though I know it could get me pregnant.

I don't care anymore.

All I want is to feel him inside me, over and over again, connecting with him until we can only exist together.

"F-F-uuuck." The long-drawn-out groan brings a smile to my face as he bursts deep inside me. I keep bouncing up and down on top of him until he's satiated and sighs with relief.

Suddenly, he cups my ass and stands up with me in his arms, his cock still deep inside me.

"Whoa, what are you d—?"

I can't even finish my sentence because he immediately steps out of the tub, clutching me with one arm as the other grabs a towel hanging from the Hook. He drapes it over us, softly caressing my skin before waltzing out of the bathroom and straight toward the bedroom.

"But we're still wet," I say.

"So?" he retorts. He places me down on the pillow, his dick still nestled inside as though he wants to stay there. And something about the way he scooped me up and placed me down on the pillow, then curled up beside me, dragging me toward him in a possessive manner, makes my whole body heat.

"Hmm …" he groans. "There is *nothing* better than this."

Now I'm blushing even more. "Nothing?"

"No," he says. "Not even sex."

I gasp and laugh at the same time. "That's hard to believe, coming from you."

He snorts, and his dick briefly pulses inside me, reminding me of his hold over me and just how much I enjoy being the object of his desires.

"You've always seemed so … sexual to me." Just saying it out loud makes me rub my lips together like I'm saying something dirty.

"There's more to me than just sex," he replies.

I turn my head. "Oh, sorry, I didn't mean to imply there wasn't. I just—"

He places a finger on my lips. "No more sorry."

After a while, I nod.

"Good girl."

Oh God. When he says it like that, it makes me want to do literally anything and everything he demands. No questions asked.

"You want to know about me? Ask," he says.

I ponder it over for a moment. "But I don't even know where to start. There's so much I don't know." I try to shift around, but his cock is still firmly lodged inside me, making me viscerally aware of how much of my body I have given him.

To this man who swooped into my life and stole it away just for the sake of freedom.

Something that should be so cruel, yet I have nothing

but intense compassion for him.

I slowly twist around.

"Wait," he says, and I stop.

His eyes close. "I don't want to stop feeling you," he groans.

The blush spreads all over my face now. "I won't pull it out."

After a few seconds, he nods, and I complete my spin around until I'm face-to-face with him, his dick still throbbing against my walls. Like an always-present reminder of his obsession with me.

My hand slides across the scars on his body and the one on his face. My finger gently traces each line, watching his every move so I don't aggravate him.

"Do they still hurt?"

He shakes his head.

"How did you get these?" I ask.

"A long time ago. From my trainer." He places his hand over mine, tracing the line of the gnarly-looking scar that runs all the way over his face. "This one."

I gulp. "Why? Why would your trainer do this to you?"

"To make me compliant," he says, his face darkening. "To punish me for ever trying to protect the only thing I cared about."

***

BEAST

Past, Age 15

I throw the knife as fast as I can, striking the man in the arm.

He yelps in pain. "Please, stop!" he begs, wriggling around in the ropes that bind him.

I throw another one right at his leg.

"Faster!"

I try not to wince as the whip strikes down on my back.

I've gotten used to pain, but the sound? The sound as it flicks through the air is what gets me.

It instills a kind of fear no one could ever understand.

"Did you hear me, you little beast?" my trainer growls.

WHACK!

Another sizzling strike. But I push on, regardless of the pain.

Another throw. Finally, I hit my target. His eye.

The man shrieks in horror as he bounces up and down in his seat. "My eye, my eye!"

"Good," my trainer says.

Just that one word gives me so much relief that I sigh out loud.

"Next target."

I suck in a breath and move on to the next victim, tied

with wrists above his head to the ceiling.

"Aim for his crotch this time."

I obey my trainer as I always do because if I don't, there is something far worse waiting for me than the lashes his whip applies.

I throw two knives. One misses. The other one hits him in the thigh.

WHACK! WHACK!

"When are you going to learn?" my trainer growls.

The disappointment in his voice hurts almost as much as the strikes do. Because if I don't appease him, if I don't learn to be a perfect killer, I may never be free from these chains.

"You can shoot a gun like a professional, yet you still can't perfectly aim a fucking knife on the first throw," he says.

WHACK!

"Yes, sir," I hiss through the pain.

"Throw!"

I do what he says and hit the man in the crotch. He shrieks in complete panic and wets himself as the blood begins to flow down his legs.

"Good. Seems pain is your only motivation," my trainer says. "I'll be sure to mention it when you're sold."

Sold.

I swallow.

The one word that should strike fear into any kid's heart. But in mine, it only brings unbridled excitement.

Being sold means a new owner, a new task, and a new way to buy my life back. The only thing I've ever truly wanted since I was stolen off the streets is my freedom.

"Come," my trainer barks, and I follow him out of the butcher's room.

Walking down a bunch of hallways, we pass the one room I hate the most out of all the rooms in this building—the one with the electric chair.

Electricity is a kind of pain the body instills as a memory, and it keeps me from ever going up against the ones who took me and made me into what I am today.

I've felt that pain so many times I can't count the number of times I begged them to stop.

When we pass it again, a weight lifts off my shoulder, and I breathe out a sigh of relief.

Not today.

Not tomorrow.

Not ever again.

As long as I … obey.

We walk past more doors, some with screeching people behind it, but I pay no attention. We head into a hallway and down to another side of the building, where there is a giant hall filled with beds. Beds meant for kids like me.

There used to be a hundred. Now only ten of us are left.

"Sleep well. More training tomorrow. Be ready and be perfect. You'll be sold tomorrow," my trainer muses.

I gasp and turn to face him. "Tomorrow already?"

He shoves me forward, paying no attention to the hint

of happiness on my face at the thought of getting out of this hellhole.

"Go to bed. I'll see you in the morning for a final training session."

"Yes, sir," I reply and go to my bunk bed.

But as soon as he's out the door, I immediately move to the wall closest to my bed, fish one leftover knife from my pocket, and go to work on the wall. Some of my fellow bunkies wake up and stare at me, but I pay no attention to them as I pry out one of the stones.

A tiny dried-up flower is hidden inside, but I handle it with utmost care as I pull it out and stare at it like it's a gift sent down from heaven.

Because this little piece of life after death reminds me that there is still hope every day.

Hope beyond these walls, beyond this life I've been thrusted into.

Hope … and a promise.

That one day, I'm going to find the one who gave this to me.

"What the fuck are you doing?"

His voice is enough to bring chills to my spine.

"Is that … a flower?" my trainer mutters.

I quickly push it back into the wall and cover it with the stone, but I'm not quick enough. My trainer shoves me aside and attempts to break it open. I do the only thing I can think of; I lunge at him.

"What the—You fucking stupid little kid!" he roars, and

he pulls out his knife and kicks at me to get me to let go of his leg. "Release me!"

But I refuse.

There is nothing on this earth I wouldn't do to keep that flower safe.

Because it's my only reminder of something beyond these walls, these chains, this visceral pain as my trainer shoves the knife into my shoulder.

I roar out loud, releasing him for a second before I shove him aside with everything I've got. Then I stand and block the wall where the flower lies.

"You … You dare to defy me?" my trainer says through gritted teeth.

Fellow bunkies watch in awe, clutching their beds like they're waiting … waiting for me to revolt.

My trainer pulls out his whip too.

"I will only say this once …" my trainer growls. "Get out of my way."

"No," I retort.

WHACK!

The whip cracks down on my chest with ease, but the pain is unlike anything else.

"MOVE!" my trainer barks.

But I stay put, guarding the only thing that matters to me in this life of pain.

Again and again, the whip comes down on me until I feel nothing but the burning sizzle of the marks he left on me.

"OBEY!" he roars, each whack harder than the one before.

But I do not relent.

Just like he taught me to in the face of pain.

After a while, he stops, and the gashes feel like smoldering paths left by volcanic ash.

My trainer breathes heavily as he pushes the whip back underneath his belt, only to lift the knife up in the air.

"What's it worth to you, little shit?" he growls. "A flap of your skin? Your tongue? Your eye?"

I don't respond.

And the knife slices through my face, all across my eyebrow and cheeks, narrowly missing my eye, only to cut into my skin like butter, splitting my face in two.

I hiss in pain but stand tall, arms still wide, ready to take whatever he needs to give me to make me suffer. To remind me of my place.

When he's done, blood drips down onto the floor. My blood.

A heavy price to pay.

While his chest rises and falls with every breath, he simply stares at me, his eyes flashing with a peculiar kind of surprise.

"A flower … you are willing to risk it all for a fucking flower?"

I lower my head, still protecting the flower with everything I have left in me.

The knife folds underneath my chin, forcing me to look

up. "Your life?"

"I have nothing if I don't have that flower," I respond.

He cocks his head and makes a tsk sound. "Pathetic."

Then he tucks his knife back into his belt and shakes his head. "Fine. Keep that dried-up piece of wilted grass." He spits on the floor in front of me. "Live with this fucking scar as a reminder of your disobedience."

"Yes, sir," I say through gritted teeth.

He kicks me in the stomach, making me buck and heave, but I continue to clutch the wall to make sure no one touches my precious gift.

"And clean up the fucking mess you made. I want this place spick-and-span by morning. I don't care how long it takes you or if you get no sleep at all." He turns around and walks out of the room, slamming the door shut behind him.

The other trainees all look at me like I've lost my mind.

"What?" I bark at them.

They all scurry off to bed like rats running for cover.

And when there's no one left to judge me, I simply turn and watch over the tiny little flower resting in that small nook inside the wall.

Even if my face and body are now marred for life … it was worth it.

Fourteen

Aurora

Present

His story moves me so much it brings me to tears.

His hand rises to meet my face, and he touches the droplets with his thumb. "Why are you crying?"

"You got this scar … because of that flower. Because of me."

He tips my chin up, making me look at him. "I got this scar because I *chose* to protect that flower. It was important to me, more important than life itself." He grabs my hand and brings it to his chest, right where his heart is. "I *choose* to protect what I care about. You."

Now it's even more impossible to stop the waterworks.

And I lean in to press a soft but powerful kiss on his lips, hoping I can say what it means to me without words.

All of his pain, all of his sacrifices, led him to this moment.

Led him to me.

And even if it's wrong, I still feel grateful.

Grateful that in all of his suffering, he found his way back to me.

***

We sleep through the days and the nights, waking only to kiss, make love, eat, and shower. Our days are spent resting and recovering from our wounds, both physical and mental. Every night I wake up drenched in sweat, only to realize I'm safe in his broad arms nestled around me like a cocoon.

He protects me as if I'm the only thing that matters to him in this entire world, and something about that makes me feel so special. So … loved.

And it's a kind of love I haven't experienced before. What I look like doesn't seem to matter anymore—only what I do, my intentions, my emotions.

Is this what life could've been like if I hadn't been born into my father's world?

I swallow away the lump in my throat as I fill a cup of fresh water from the sink.

Every sip reminds me that I can never take something as simple as water for granted. Or food.

We don't have much, but we've made do with what was still there from previous vacations. Before my life was replaced by one I barely even recognize.

Just like the girl staring back at me when I look in the tiny mirror hanging on the wall in the hallway.

There's something about her, something about me, that's changed.

That girl no longer wants to hide.

She has this kind of … courage.

And it scares me.

I put down my glass and approach Beast, who stares at himself in the mirror, his fingers tracing his scars. He's wearing only a towel, and it's so damn hard not to gape at his rigged muscles, especially knowing what he can do with them.

"What are you doing?" I ask.

Our eyes connect through the mirror. He tilts his head and touches the base of his neck. "I need this thing … out of me."

I rub my lips together. Right. The device Lex uses to keep him under control.

"But I can't reach it myself," he says, staring at me intently.

Oh God. He wants me to do it?

My stomach drops.

"Aurora." The way he says my name makes goose

bumps scatter on my skin. "Help me."

Wow.

He's never asked me for help.

And it almost sounded like ... begging.

How can I say no to that?

When he turns, I feel queasy.

I swallow and nod, but the more I think about it, the more anxious I get.

He walks past me and heads straight into the kitchen, fishing one of the bigger knives from the cupboard. "This should do the trick."

My eyes widen at the size of that thing. "You want me to ... cut you with that?"

With a nod, he pushes the knife into my hands, then sits down on the stool and stares at me like I'm wasting time.

I gulp and approach him, but the closer I get, the more nervous I become.

Oh God. Am I really going to do this? Can I really cut into someone's flesh?

"Sanitize it," he says. "With fire."

I nod and carry it to the stove. Turning on the burner, I heat the blade so it's sterile. Then I stand behind him. He tilts his head even farther to the side, exposing the skin where there's an obvious scar. "There." His breath is steady, while mine is completely unhinged.

Sweat drops trickle down my forehead. "I don't know if I can do this."

"Yes, you can," he says, eyeing me from the side. "I

believe in you."

His words bring me a little bit of courage, but when I sit down behind him and actually point the knife at his back, I get cold feet.

"What if I mess up?" I say. "I don't want to hurt you."

"Hey," he says with a low voice. "You can do this. I trust you."

I touch his hot skin, sweat drops trickling down my face as I put the knife at the edge of the device. I can feel it move underneath his skin.

"Don't hesitate. I can take it," he says.

And I puncture his skin.

The blood runs out immediately, covering his back, but he seems unfazed, so I cut farther, deeper into his skin. It feels odd, like cutting into Jell-O, and the warm blood covering the blade makes me even more nauseous than before.

He hisses as I slice farther, making an opening. "I'm sorry," I mutter.

"Don't. Just take it out," he says through gritted teeth.

I carve it out farther until I finally see the chip. "There."

I put the knife aside and lean in with my nails, tugging at one of the edges until it dislodges from his body. He groans as I pull out and chuck it onto the floor.

"Oh my God …" I mutter, staring at the device.

Beast stands up and crushes it underneath his foot, rage almost boiling his skin. "Never again."

I just stare at him with bloodied fingers and a stomach

ready to flip over.

God, I can't believe I just did that.

I actually cut something out of his flesh.

I run to the bathroom to clean my hands and wash away the blood. When I return, his back is still covered in blood, so I quickly fetch the first-aid kit from the shelves again. After grabbing a few sterile tissues and some alcohol to pat down the wound, I tape it all up neatly and clean up his back too.

He just stands there, silently letting me do my thing.

He turns to face me. "Thank you." He puts so much emphasis on the words that I don't even know how to respond. It's as though he wants to instill me with his gratitude.

I breathe out a sigh of relief and clean the knife, then put it back where it belongs.

With my hands leaning on the counter, I close my eyes and take another deep breath.

That was heavy.

Suddenly, his hands wrap around my waist, and he plants a sweet but sultry kiss on my shoulder. "I would be nothing without you."

It's hard to swallow but even harder to breathe.

"You … you're a living, walking god. And I'm just tiny little me."

He snorts. "Tiny … I like that new nickname."

I smile and shake my head. "No."

"Yes."

"No."

"Yes," he keeps insisting.

I snort. "We almost sound like a boring old couple arguing now. And no, absolutely not 'tiny.'"

"Maybe I'd like to be a boring old couple," he muses, pressing another kiss to my shoulder. "Beauty."

The thought makes my heart flutter.

But could we have such a future together?

Suddenly, my stomach roars.

And he definitely noticed, judging from the frown on his face. "You're hungry."

"It's fine," I reply. I take a much-needed sip of my water and check our cupboards. There are only a few pieces of bread left and some jam in the fridge. Just one more day.

I sigh.

"What's wrong?" Beast asks.

"We're running out of food," I reply.

"Well, we can get more," he says.

I place my cup down. "How? We don't have any money."

He shrugs. "Steal it."

I frown. "No. That's wrong."

He snorts and points at himself. "I've lived as a criminal."

I make a face. "Well, it doesn't have to be that way. We could try something else."

"How?" he says, tilting his head. "Beg for food?"

I roll my eyes. "No, I mean like … shouldn't we go find

some jobs?"

His face grows tighter, darker, more intense. Like all the joy has been sucked out of him. "No."

A pang hits my stomach. "Why not?"

What's wrong with a regular job?

"Have you seen me?" he replies with a furrowed brow.

"Yes. Of course. That doesn't have to mean anything." It's hard not to look at him, that's for sure, especially when he wears so little that I can practically look underneath.

"No, no way," he says, shaking his head.

I sigh out loud. "C'mon. We need to figure something out. We can't stay here if we don't do something to get money."

"Stealing works too," he says, grabbing a cup. "I won't hurt anyone."

"If you steal once, what are you going to do next? Steal again?" I fold my arms. "Forever and ever?"

"Whatever it takes," he says like it's the most normal thing in the world.

"I don't want to be like that. I want to be a good and honest person," I say.

He fills his cup with water and stares at me with a raised brow. "Not everything in life is good and honest." He takes a big gulp.

"Just because we've been thrust into a bad life," I respond, "doesn't mean we have to stick with it."

He puts his cup down on the counter and gazes at it for a second. "I don't know how to do anything else."

My face softens. His life was nothing short of cruel, and I understand why he thinks he wouldn't be able to.

"All I've known is how to steal. Hunt. Kill. Just to survive," he adds, clutching the counter like it hurts him to even think about it.

"But you had a life before you lived on the streets too." I place a hand on his chest where his heart is. "You were a good person then, and you're still a good person now."

His eyes home in on mine, searching for something, but I don't know what. It's almost as if he's digging into his own memories.

"I don't know …" he mutters, and he quickly looks away.

"There must be something you remember. Something you used to love doing. Maybe we can look at something like that," I say, hoping to find a way in.

Because if I give up now … what hope do we have of even a semblance of a normal life together?

He walks off, but I push back the anxiety and follow him to the living room.

"Don't shut me out, Beast." I follow him to the window, where he stares out at the busy street. "Please."

His fist tightens. "My life before I was taken, before I became an orphan … it's all a blur."

My brows draw together, and I can't help but lean in to place a hand on his shoulder. "I'm sorry. I didn't know it was still that painful."

He places his hand over mine, squeezing gently. "I have

nothing, no money, no clothes, no home. Only you." When he turns to look at me, the agony in his eyes makes me swallow back the tears. "And I want nothing more than to protect you. But I don't even know who I am without fighting. Without that collar and these scars." He gazes at his own hands and chest like it's the first time he's actually looking, really looking, at his own wounds.

I gently move in to stand in front of him so he can't look anywhere else but at me, and I place my hand on his face. "You can be so much more than what they made you."

"How? When I don't even remember who I was before?" he says.

His misery cuts into my soul like a knife. I've never felt this kind of pain before, so visceral, so … profound.

"But you weren't called 'Beast' to begin with, right?"

He shakes his head. "I don't remember."

"Nothing?" But when he closes his eyes, the answer is clear.

I wrap my arms around him and hug him tight. "I want to help you remember."

"Why?"

I lean away to look into his eyes. "So we can find the boy hidden deep inside this killer's body," I say, pointing at his chest. "Because I know he's still in there, somewhere."

He grabs my fingers tight. "That boy … was left behind the day his parents died."

"Then we will find him there," I reply.

His brows twitch. "What are you thinking?"

I grab his hand and drag him along. "Let's go."

"Aurora," he growls but still lets me tag him along.

"We're going back to where it all started. Back to the place we first met," I say. "Your parents' apartment."

I hop into the car and wait until he's in the driver's seat.

"This is dangerous," he grumbles in a low tone.

I shrug. "Only my father knows about that place. No one will look for us there."

Despite his reservations, Beast sits down and fastens his seat belt. "I hope you know what you're getting yourself into."

"No," I reply with courage, just like he taught me. If he can see beauty in me, I want him to see the beauty in him, too. "But not knowing who you are is no way to live either. So let's go."

Fifteen

BEAST

Seeing the building where I was born makes my feet feel glued to the ground.

I can only look up at one spot; the window on the fifth floor. It's blocked off with shoddy wood that looks half-rotten. Old.

"Are you ready?" Aurora's voice is like a bullet hitting me in the dark, immediately drawing my attention. Rain pitter-patters down onto her head. "Let's go inside."

She clutches my hand, weaving her three fingers through

mine. Slowly, she pulls me along with her, into the building, into the place where my nightmares began.

She leads me inside and up the staircase. But the higher we go, the more my entire body begins to sweat.

It's as if I'm walking right back into my past, my memories coming to life.

My hands clutch the banister, but it feels cold to the touch, and when I lift it, I swear there's a droplet of blood.

"Are you okay?" Aurora asks.

When I look again, the blood is gone.

As if it never even existed.

Am I hallucinating?

I nod at Aurora even though it's a lie, but I don't want her to worry.

I've never been anything but strong, and I refuse to stop now.

"Which number was it?" she asks, narrowing her eyes at all the doors in the hallway.

I point at the one on the far end. "That one."

She grabs my hand and walks with me to the door. "C'mon. We can do this."

She opens it up. It's still unlocked, covered in police tape. But there's no sign of life inside the apartment.

Every piece of furniture is still there—upturned, thrown aside, broken down—left exactly the way the police found it. As if suspended in time.

No one has been here since that night. Not one soul dared to purchase the property, probably assuming it's haunted by the memory of the violence that took place there.

I push away the restlessness building in my muscles and step into the rubble of what was once my life before my parents died. Before I became an orphan, forced to survive out on the streets, eating nothing but scraps until I was picked up by snatchers and taken into a strict training facility. All so I could be made into the perfect weapon. A killing machine. A man known only as Beast.

What was left of the boy I was before doesn't exist anymore. Every trace of him has been erased off the face of this earth.

I push open a door and see a bloodied mark on the floor near the bed.

BANG!

The gunshot goes off in my mind. I can still hear it.

Along with my mother's screams.

I go to my knees in front of the blood and touch it.

This … this is all that's left of her.

Aurora stays behind in the living room, rubbing her lips together without saying a word. But who would know what to say when faced with this kind of cruelty? No one.

This is the kind of misery that would turn any man into a monster.

A monster such as me.

Suddenly, I notice the teddy bear lying on the bed. Eyes glazy, fur covered in dust, but its bow still wrapped tightly around its neck.

I step over the blood and grab the bear off the bed, staring at it for a while.

And for the first time in forever, I hear my mother's voice, speaking to me in a language I've forgotten how to use.

***

Age 7

"And the little bear made its way back home to momma and papa bear, who happily welcomed him back into their arms with a hug," my mom says, finishing the story.

She puts the bear underneath my blanket like she always does. "Slaap lekker, lief engeltje van me."

She rarely talks in her native language, but when she does, I always appreciate it even though I don't speak it myself. My father pushed me to go to an English school very early on. He always told me it was so we could return to America one day.

But I know some of the words she's spoken. Because lief engeltje means sweet angel, and it makes me smile.

When she gets up from the bed, I say, "Mom?"

"Yes, honey?" She turns to face me. "What's the matter?"

"Will you and Dad always be here with me?" I ask.

The look on her face fills with worry, and she clutches her own fingers. "Of course, honey." She puts her hand over my chest. "Even when we're not physically with you, we will always be here. Inside your heart."

"Inside me?" I mutter, and she nods. "But what if you get locked inside?"

She giggles. "No silly, not like that."

"Then how do you get out?" I ask.

She laughs and kisses me on the forehead. "I'll explain it to you when you're older. It's time for sleep now."

I huddle underneath the blanket with my little bear as she tucks me in.

"Sleep tight, little angel." She gives me another peck and turns off the light before she leaves.

And for a few minutes, everything is quiet, peaceful, just like how it always is.

BANG!

The loud shot jolts me into an upright position, and I gasp for air, my heart thundering as loudly as that blast just now.

What was that?

Suddenly, my mom storms back into the room.

"Mom? What's wrong?"

"No time," she mutters. She crawls under the bed and grabs the gun they never keep loaded.

Until she finally fishes a box from the top shelves of the closet and puts the bullets inside herself.

"Mom, what's happening?" I ask. "You're scaring me."

"Go to the bathroom," she says, her voice more anxious than I've ever heard. "Hide."

"What? Why?" I say, yawning. "I thought it was time to sl—"

"NOW!" she growls right in my face.

I gulp back the fear and tears.

"And be quiet. Don't make a sound." She puts her fingers over her lips. "No matter what you hear, do not come out. Okay?"

I nod a few times, trying to understand.

"I know it's hard, but you gotta do what I tell you, okay?" she adds, and she adds another kiss. "Now go."

I don't wait for another second as I run out of the bedroom and into the bathroom. I close the door and hide inside the bathtub, then pull the curtains.

I'm shivering. Cold. Tired. Panicking all alone.

Don't make a sound. Don't make a sound.

BANG!

I cover my ears with my hands and make myself as small as possible, hiding in the corner of this bath, praying no one will find me here.

But nothing prepares me for my mother's scream.

It's so loud and high pitched that it enters my lungs and makes me hold my breath.

What's happening to her and Papa? What's going on?

I can't move. Momma told me to stay here and hide, no matter how hard it gets, even though I really want to go out there and help her.

But how long should I stay?

Suddenly, the door opens.

I hold my breath and stay frozen to the bathtub.

The toilet seat is lifted, and it sounds like someone is puking.

I really want to peek, but I force myself to remain still, guarded and vigilant.

But a tiny sliver of the curtain isn't closed, and I can see past it through the mirror where a girl with flowing black hair and pristine white skin is washing her face.

And our eyes connect.

My heart skips a beat.

I blink.

Just once.

But it's enough to break my world.

The curtain is slowly peeled away, and my secret hiding spot is no longer secret.

Two big brown eyes stare into mine, coral lips slowly twitching up into a smile.

What am I supposed to do?

Is she the enemy my mom and dad always warned me about?

The girl plucks at the small pink flower in her hair and gives it to me, tucking it into my hand like she wants to tell me something.

Give me the one thing that's slipped away from me ever since my mother told me to go and hide, no matter what I would hear.

Hope.

***

Present

"I remember this," I say, staring at the bathtub at the far end of the bathroom, clutching the bear so tight it almost rips open.

Aurora peeks along with me. "The bear?"

I turn to face her. "You."

Her face flushes with heat. "I …"

I pull the flower out of my pocket and hold it up between us. "This. This is what kept me going for all these years."

Tears well up in her eyes. "I didn't know what else to do."

"You gave me a purpose." I grab her hand and push the flower inside. "Something to fight for."

She looks up at me with those same doe-like eyes she gave me the first time we met, but I'm no longer that terrified little boy I once was. Through hardship and pain, I endured. Through sheer willpower, I became what I needed when no one was there to save me.

I didn't suffer all those years just to destroy.

I lived through misery so I could find my way back to her.

So I could give her what she gave me.

Protection.

I wrap her in my arms and pull her close, hugging her with everything I have. "Your father didn't find me because of you. Your kindness saved me."

She puts her head on my shoulder, and we stay there for a moment, basking in the comfort of our collective pain, knowing we have each other when everything else has crumbled all around us.

I don't need money, I don't need a job, or even a home … as long as I have her.

"But we didn't even find out your name," she mutters after a while, still holding me tight.

"I did," I reply.

She pulls back and stares into my eyes with wonder in hers. "How?"

I hold up the teddy bear and show her the bloodied piece of fabric that has the washing instructions on it. In tiny letters, a name is scribbled on top, in case the teddy ever got lost.

Jax.

Sixteen

Aurora

Not one second does he let go of my hand as we drive all the way back to the beach house. I can't stop glancing at him to catch a glimpse of the man who finally has a name.

Jax.

I repeat it in my head, but it still doesn't feel real.

This is the name of the guy I spent all this time with in that damn cell, yet it's still difficult to fathom he is the same person I once saved from my father's wrath.

The pink hue of the flower's petals peek through the opening of his pocket, a forever reminder of our connection.

But is it enough?

I swallow and turn to look at the beach house as the car stops in the driveway.

I feel like our whole world has stood still since we returned to his childhood home, yet the sun is still shining, and the people are still bustling around the streets like nothing even happened.

"What's wrong?" he suddenly asks.

My lips part, but I don't know how to answer. "N-Nothing."

He raises his brow at me. "Tell me. Now."

I tuck my hair behind my ear. "It … It feels so different to come back here now."

With his arm resting on the steering wheel, he turns to me. "Why?"

"I don't know… like the people are still going about their day, while ours feels so … out of this world."

He leans in, his hand slowly cupping my face and caressing my cheek with his thumb in a way that warms my heart. "Your heart is too big for your tiny body."

I frown, confused. "What do you mean?"

"You care too much about people who don't matter," he says, and he places a kiss on my forehead.

I blush and smile. "So what do we do now? We just go back to the cabin and pretend nothing happened?"

"What do you mean?"

"Well, I don't even know what to call you," I say, biting my lip. "I know you as Beast, but your name is Jax, and I don't know which one you prefer."

He rests his forehead against mine, staring into my soul with those penetrative emerald eyes. "Beast. Jax. As long as it's your voice calling, I'll answer."

God. The blush on my cheeks turns an even brighter shade of red than before.

"But Lex called you Beast to show his power over you. It doesn't feel right."

He clutches my face with both hands. "I am what I am. A name doesn't change that."

I nod a couple of times.

"Now call me …" he murmurs.

I'm drowning in those beautiful eyes of his. "Beast."

The smirk that follows makes my heart flutter. "Say it again."

"Beast."

His eyes close, and he groans, almost as if he's getting fired up. As though this horrible word that used to contain him and keep him prisoner now brings him power. Just because of my voice.

"I am your beast …" he says, licking his top lip. "And I will always be."

I smile. "Even if I call you Jax sometimes?"

"Even then." He opens the door and adds, "C'mon, let's go."

He gets out of the car, and with a sigh to calm down my lusty heart, I hop out too.

While he fishes some supplies out of the back of the car we picked up from his old house, I go inside. A strange, musty smell permeates the living room, and it makes me pause to sniff where it's coming from. Did I leave something open on the kitchen counter? How? There wasn't much food, to begin with. What we had was left from past vacations.

But it doesn't smell like food either … it smells like … unwashed ass.

Suddenly, something shuffles near the stove.

My eyes widen, and I pick up a nearby candleholder and raise it over my head as a weapon.

My heart rate picks up speed as I approach whatever is making the sound in the corner.

It sounds like a rat, scurrying across the floor, searching for scraps. But the closer I get, the bigger it becomes. And when a pair of pants come into view, I know for sure.

It's human.

I shriek.

A head rises. Two eyes meet mine.

Someone bursts in through the door behind me. "Aurora?!"

"Papa?!" I yell.

My father is looking at me with widened eyes as though he's as surprised as I am that he's here in this house.

Beast clutches my shoulders and pushes me aside, ready to attack, but I grab his arm, barely able to hold him back. "No, no, don't."

"You?!" Beast growls out loud.

My father slowly comes to a rise, his hands still covered

in the crumbs of the crackers he found in one of the bottom drawers.

"What are you doing here?" Beast snarls at him.

My father stares at both of us, raising his brows in a demeaning manner. "I could ask you two the same thing. This is *my* beach house."

He eyes me up and down. "What are you trying to do? Pummel me with a candle?" He snorts.

"I thought you were one of Lex's men," I say, quickly lowering the holder. "I didn't know it was you down there. What are you even doing here?" I mutter, completely taken aback.

"What does it look like?" He pats his hands on his pants. "Trying to find some food and shelter. Obviously, it's too late, it seems. Goddammit. Of course, even my last hideout goes up in smoke."

Beast still marches toward him, escaping my grasp, and grabs him by the collar. "Did you bring them here?"

"Who?" my father splutters.

"Lex's guards!" Beast grits.

"No, of course not," my father retorts. "I'm not Aurora. I actually keep an eye out on my surroundings."

Why does he always have to turn everything into an insult?

Beast releases his collar and shoves him down on the floor.

"Jesus Christ," my father says, coughing.

I quickly go to my knees in front of him and check him for wounds, but my father only has eyes for Beast.

"Where the hell are your manners, you animal!?" my father growls.

"Manners?" Beast sneers back, making a fist. "You are the last person on this planet to know what they are."

"I beg your pardon?" My father's brows draw together. "You literally tried to kill my daughter and me several times!"

"You didn't care if she died as long as it saved your ass!" Beast roars, getting up in his face.

I push back both of them with a hand on their chests, separating them as best as I can. "Please, guys."

But I don't seem to be getting through to either of them. Their eyes are homed in on each other as if they plan to throw knives at each other's throats. Beast glances at the kitchen drawer that contains them.

"Beast," I hiss as I get up to block the drawer. "Don't."

"How did you find us?" he snarls at my father.

"I didn't even know you two would be here," my father replies.

Of course, he wasn't looking for me.

But why does this admission still sting deep inside my heart?

"Why are you even here?" he asks.

"This was the only safe place I could think of," I say.

"Well, it's not safe with *him* here," my father balks, throwing daggers at Beast with his eyes.

Beast lunges forward and grabs my father by the collar again, spitting in his face, "You're the reason she's been suffering all this time!"

"Beast!" I yell, pushing him away. "Stop."

His eyes find mine in the dark, a glimmer of hope flashing through. "I would rip out his tongue and feed it to him just for hurting you."

Tears well up in my eyes, but I swallow them back down. "I know."

His nostrils flare, and for a moment, I worry he might actually go through with it. But then he drops my father to the floor and marches to the living room, where he sits down on the couch, seething with rage.

I thank him with my eyes and take in a deep breath, then focus on my father.

"Thank you," he mutters.

"Yeah, don't," I reply, helping him up from the floor.

"What?"

"Thank me," I reply.

He throws me a damning look. "What's that supposed to mean?"

"You know what it means," I say. "Don't pretend you don't know you hurt me."

He sucks in a breath and straightens his back, posturing. "Well, I did what I did because I had to. Do you think I had any other choice, strapped to that chair?"

"Well …" I don't even know how to answer because I know the things a person is pushed to do when faced with death. I tried to sell out my father just to get out.

Doesn't that make me just as much of an awful person as he is?

"Exactly." My father steps forward, closer toward Beast. "You're still my daughter, even when you don't want to be. And this is my house, my hideout, whether either of you likes it or not," he says. "The only one Lex didn't find, apparently. No thanks to you, of course."

"Papa, stop," I tell him as he approaches Beast. "Please."

"No, all of this happened because *he* came to our house." He points at Beast like he's the unwanted one. "Because *he* tried to murder us."

He's full-on raging now, and Beast is just sitting there, oozing in rage. I can tell he's holding himself back, physically restraining himself against the couch, nails digging into the fabric as though they're claws meant to restrain him.

"I could've given you the money. It was right there in the warehouse, waiting for your fucking owner. You could've taken it back to him, and we could've lived our life in peace," my father rants. "Instead, you chose to make our lives a living hell."

Beast's fingers push into the couch so hard they almost break as he stands up, towering over my father with a kind of fury that could wake a sleeping volcano.

"What choice!?" Beast yells out loud. He tilts his head and shows my father the scar on his neck. "He implanted a fucking torture device. This is how he kept me on a ball and chain."

"I don't see anything—"

"Because your daughter cut it out of me!"

"Gross," my father mutters.

Beast steps forward. "You want me to make you feel how gross I can get?!"

I swallow away the lump in my throat. "PLEASE!"

My voice makes them both stop.

"Papa, please, believe him. Lex literally electrocuted him. I saw it myself several times. It hurt him so much that it forced him to obey."

My father turns up his nose. "Still … pain shouldn't be the only measure to make a decision."

"You were willing to sacrifice *her* to save your own life," Beast growls back, pointing at me.

"That's what comes with the world we live in, the business I do," my father says. "You have no clue what kind of pressure I'm under to maintain—"

"I KNOW!" Beast growls, his voice heavier than I've ever heard before. "I *know* you."

My father frowns. "Well, I don't know you, yet you keep involving yourself in our business. You're free now. Why don't you just run away and leave us be?"

"Because *she* saved me," Beast says, fishing the flower from his pocket to show it to my father. "She gave this to me …" He narrows his eyes at my father. "The night you killed my parents."

My father's pupils dilate, and he takes a step back. "What …?" He looks at me, searching for answers, but I don't even know what to say. "When?"

Beast's face darkens. "I was the boy who escaped."

My father's face slowly loses all its color as he begins to realize the magnitude of his actions. Of everything that led us to this moment, this place.

"It's you … you're the reason behind all of my misery."

Seventeen

Aurora

My. Misery.

Not a single second did he think of me.

My fingers clench around the candleholder so harshly that it almost snaps in two.

Suddenly, my father runs to the kitchen and takes out a huge butcher's knife. Beast runs toward me, but my father pokes it between us.

"Stay away!" he snaps, lashing out at Beast.

Beast jumps sideways and narrowly avoids every strike, but my father keeps slashing away wildly. My father almost manages to cut the flower, but Beast keeps it at arm's length like it's the most precious thing he's guarding. Neither of them relents.

"Stop!" I yell, but they both ignore me.

Beast grabs my father's wrist mid-swing and knocks the knife from his hand, but he keeps twisting it until he begins to shriek in pain. "Ow, ow, ow!"

"Stop it!" I yell, trying to separate them, but I can't get through.

"Let me go, you beast!" my father growls, punching at him with every bit of strength he has left. But none of them seem to faze Beast even the slightest as he grabs the knife and holds it over my father's throat.

"Beg," Beast says through gritted teeth.

"Please, Beast, Papa … stop," I beg, my eyes growing even more teary. "Enough is enough. You are both family."

Now they both look at me like I've gone insane.

"No," my father barks at me, and he jerks himself free from Beast's grip before crawling away on the floor like a wounded animal. He points at Beast. "That *thing* is not family."

"He's a human being, just like you and me," I say.

My father's gaze is solely on Beast. "Letting you escape was the worst mistake I ever made. I should've killed you when I had the chance!"

"Yes, you should have," Beast retorts, lowering his eyes. "Because I will never, ever stop trying to make you pay for what you did to her."

My father's in shock for a moment before he rebukes, "What I did? What about you? You tried to abduct her and kill her!"

"No!" I interject. "He tried to save me."

"By bringing you to that cell?" he spits.

"My orders were to kill everyone on sight," Beast says, tucking the flower back into his pocket. "It was the only way."

My father scoffs. "Maybe you should've killed her. At least it would've saved her from all this pain."

Beast's eyes are filled with rage. "*You* made her suffer all that pain by lending all that money and not paying it back!"

Papa rebukes, "Because I was trying to fix her."

Beast roars like a madman. "She's not broken! She's perfect!"

I stumble backward, dropping the candleholder. My hand rises to meet my eyes as I stare at the one thing that's brought about so much misery in this world. These scars, these malformed hands, this body that destroyed my mother's ... me. I'm the reason my father had to pay, had to be killed, why I was taken, why Beast was snatched and trained, why everyone is the way they are now.

And it suddenly feels like I can't breathe.

Beast stomps toward my father, who cowers in the corner of the living room.

"The only reason you're still alive is because I protected you," Beast growls at my father, pointing at him. "Because she loves you, and I love her."

"*Love?*" my father splutters. "Do you even know what that is?"

"I know more about love than you ever will," Beast replies, tapping my father's chest.

I can tell it takes every ounce of self-control in him not to snap my father's neck.

My father shakes his head, fuming with rage. "I sacrificed *everything* for her." He glances at me now. "You are *my* daughter, Aurora. And I will do what I need to protect my family."

"Family …" I mutter.

It's something I've always wanted but never truly knew.

"We're family, Aurora," my father says, playing on my heartstrings.

But I know it can't be true.

I don't want her. I never did.

She's a monster.

Beast merely watches me, but the pain in his eyes is almost unbearable.

"We should stay together as a family. Us two. Not him."

What?

"He doesn't belong here, Aurora," my father continues, his tone lowering. "He's the enemy."

My heart begins to drop.

"No," I say, shaking my head.

My father's face darkens. "Are you in love with him?" my father asks.

I don't even know how to answer without feeling judged.

But my face apparently says enough because the disgust

clearly shows on his face. "Wow. You want to be with *him*?" my father says as he gets up from the floor. "He's a murderer who betrayed his own men."

"Stop," I mutter, closing my eyes because I can't stand to even look while they try to face off again.

"No, you have to choose. Him or me," he retorts.

"Don't make me do this," I beg, rubbing my lips together to stop the tears from flowing.

"Wow. I never thought this day would come. Betrayed by my own fucking daughter." My father's nostrils flare. "I can't listen to another minute of this," my father barks as he storms out the door. "Good fucking luck."

I expected Beast to follow him and throw him down to the ground to wrestle him to death.

Instead, he stands there in the living room like a giant made of stone, feet lodged firmly onto the floor. As though he's afraid that if he even moves a single inch, he might end up hurting my father. Hurting me.

Tears slowly begin to roll down my cheeks, and suddenly, he moves.

He stomps toward me and wraps me into his arms, almost crushing me in his embrace.

"Don't cry," he says.

"I can't stop," I reply. "I don't know how."

"Don't give him any of your tears," he says. "He's not worth a single one."

I hug him as tight as he's hugging me, the pressure enough to force me to stop.

"He's really gone, isn't he?" I ask.

He doesn't respond, but I can feel his chest tighten.

"I don't have anyone left," I mutter, feeling the gaping hole in my heart growing.

"You have me," he rebukes, holding on tight.

But that's just it.

I need Beast. Desperately.

But does he really need me? What can I possibly give him?

I sigh.

He pushes me away. "You're thinking too much again, aren't you?" he asks, capturing my attention with a simple stern gaze. "Tell me."

"I just …" I sigh and look away. "I feel like such a burden to everyone."

"You are *not* a burden. Forget what your father told you. It's not true."

"But everything happened because of me," I say, the words so visceral I can feel them slicing into my own heart. I step back to stop myself from falling into his arms again because I don't want to put that on him.

My guilt is mine alone to carry.

"All you've ever done is help me. How do you think I broke free from those chains?" he says, his voice lower, more intense.

I suck in a breath, stepping back when he steps forward.

"You think I got that strength out of nowhere?" he says, clutching my arm so I can't move away. "You gave it to me."

I gave him that strength? How?

"Again and again. Not just in that cell, but before too. When you helped me fight Lex. When you stopped them from electrocuting me." His grip tightens. "When you gave that flower to me."

"I wanted to save us both," I mutter. "I didn't mean to—"

"Become my only reason for existing?"

The air feels too thick to breathe.

He pulls me close to him, despite the fact that my hand is right there between us. "It's the truth." His forehead leans against mine. "I'm in love with you, Aurora."

He's said it before, and I want to believe it, but can I?

"But how? You've seen what I look like. You heard what those men … and even my own father … call me." His jaw tightens as I say the word. "Monster."

And I don't think I've ever seen him more enraged.

His eyes slowly travel down my face, all the way to his own chest, where my hand is still pressed up against him. And I become viscerally aware of just how madly he's gazing at me and my deformed fingers … at how badly I wished I still had my gloves.

"My father used all his money to fix me, and it didn't even work… I'm still a monster." I mutter, not knowing what to say.

His hand rises, and he grabs my hand, entangling his fingers through mine.

"You are *not* a monster. You're beautiful."

***

BEAST

She gasps in shock as though she cannot fathom that I'd say that word again now that I've seen what she had to hide.

Whatever she was taught to believe while growing up, it's all a lie. Made up by her lousy, thieving father who cared nothing about the daughter he was given.

But she is beautiful, she always was, and I want her to know.

"Beautiful? I…?" She can't finish her sentence. "You said that before in the cell, but I didn't believe it was true. I—"

"It was true then, and it's true now," I interrupt.

I lift her hand and bring it to my face, looking at it thoroughly. But I don't see what she sees. I don't see the monster her father made her out to be. I see the girl who went through all the pain in the world just to protect the people she loved.

I pull her hand closer and bring her fingers to my lips to kiss the tips.

Her lips part, and I can tell she's struggling to breathe.

"You're beautiful," I say, planting more and more kisses all over her fingers and hand.

"You don't have to say that," she says. "You don't have to make me feel better after—"

"I'll say it a million times more until you believe it too." I interject, pausing my kisses only to look into her eyes so she knows I mean it.

And I'll make do on my promise right now as I pull her hand closer and kiss every inch of her fingers—every ridge, every bump, every scar. All of it is beautiful because it's a part of her, and she is nothing but beauty. Not only on the outside but on the inside too. Her heart is too huge for her tiny body. She brought kindness where there was only corruption, and for that, I'll be eternally grateful.

So I kiss her with everything I have, dragging my lips along her hand and arm, snaking around her body until I'm right behind her. And I wrap my arms around her body and sink my teeth into her shoulders just like before.

"Oh God, what are you doing?" she mutters.

"Making you forget," I reply, licking up the tiny blood droplet before kissing the small wound. "Just like you made me forget in that cell."

She whimpers as I drag my mouth along her skin all the way up to her neck, leaving pecks all over. And I move her along with me, dragging her body from behind all the way to a large mirror standing in the bedroom where I force her to stand.

And together, we look at how I lick the wound on her neck, then kiss her other arm and fingers, and all the scars left behind by her past.

"I'll cover every inch of your skin with kisses until you believe me," I whisper into her ear.

Tears roll down her cheeks. "But all I've done is cause pain to the people I love."

There it is. The pain behind all the lies.

The scar she kept hidden from the world.

The lies her father made her believe.

"You are not responsible for your father's actions," I say. "Do you hear me?"

She nods.

I grab her chin and force her to look at herself in the mirror. "Did you love your mother, even when you never knew her?"

She nods again.

"She knew you too, even before you were born. Your mother made you with love." When I grab her throat, I add, "Say it."

"My mother made me with love," she says.

"She made you exactly how you were meant to be," I say, never breaking our eye contact.

"How I was meant …" she mutters. "To be."

"She made you to be loved," I say. "And your father broke that oath."

More tears roll down her cheeks.

"He. Doesn't. Deserve. You." My voice crackles with pain. "Say it."

"He doesn't deserve me," she repeats.

With every word, it's as if an invisible weight lifts off her shoulders.

"And these hands," I say, sliding my fingers down to her fingers. "Have only ever touched with kindness. They deserve to be loved. Now say you deserve it."

Her cheeks flush. "I deserve it."

"Good girl." Her cheeks only redden more.

She swallows, and her pretty pink lips tip up into a brave smile.

"And if you still think you're a monster … then we'll be monsters together," I say.

She gasps as I press another kiss right underneath her ear.

Grabbing her hand, I bring it to her chest and place it on her heart. "It's time you learned to see yourself the way I see you." I slide her hand down slowly between the crevice of her tits, all the way down to her jeans. And I quickly pop the button and pull the zipper, exposing her bare pussy since she was going commando.

I slide her hand down between her legs while staring into her eyes through the mirror, making sure she knows I see her hesitation. Her wishes. Her needs. Her fantasies. Her darkest desires. And all that makes her who she is.

All that makes me want to devour her.

And I lift a strand of hair to whisper into her ear, "Now pleasure yourself the way you like it … while I watch."

Eighteen

Aurora

While he ... watches?

The mere idea makes my entire body burst into flames.

I've only touched myself in that cell once, when I needed to entice him to free himself. But that was for an entirely different reason, and the thought of doing it now makes me anxious. Excited. Greedy.

My hands are right there, on my pussy, and he's moving them around just like he did when he was in control. Back when we were still in that cold, damp cell, willing to do anything to take us out of there.

But this, this is different.

We're unshackled now, completely free to do what we

want.

He could walk out of this door and never look back. He owes me nothing.

Yet he chooses to stay and kiss me. Hug me. Tell me I'm beautiful. Shower my body with a kind of love I've never known.

A kind of love I deserve.

My body opens up to my own touch as my legs willingly spread while he pushes down my fingers, circling around. My head tilts back against his chest as the heat starts to build.

"You feel it now, don't you?" he murmurs. "That same lust you felt when I touched you."

I can feel the wetness spreading across my own fingers, and it feels so wrong, so immoral. Everything I was thinking goes out the window as he rubs my own hand all over, putting pressure in all the right places. Slowly, I'm coming undone in the best kind of way.

"Don't look away," he says as my eyes slowly start to close.

His voice keeps me in the here and now as I struggle to even breathe from the way I'm touching myself with his help.

I've never looked at my own pussy before like this, all hot and bothered, desperate for more. And it feels so good that I don't want to stop.

He takes my earlobe into his mouth and sucks. "Every inch of your skin tastes like heaven."

I moan out loud when he nibbles a little, flicking my clit back and forth, not caring anymore if it's right or not. I want this. I want more of this. And I want all of him.

Is it okay to need someone like him?

To crave someone so desperately it feels like you can't breathe without them?

I suck in a breath when his other free hand slides up my body and grips my breast. He circles my nipple, and when he tugs at it through the shirt, I let out another moan.

"Make yourself come in front of me," he says, almost pushing me over the edge. "Look at yourself in the mirror while you fall apart."

And I can't stop staring into the mirror, no matter how dirty it feels. Dirty has never felt this good before.

His hand slowly releases mine, allowing me to explore on my own. While I try to focus on my own pleasure, a hand snakes up my belly, and I feel every hard ridge of his calloused hands as it wraps around my throat, squeezing a little. "More. Noise."

But I feel so locked up, so overwhelmed.

Until I feel his other hand, the one he used to help me, snake its way down my ass. And suddenly, he pushes inside my other hole.

I gasp, my eyes widening in shock that he'd actually go there.

"I want you," he groans. "*All* of you."

"But that's immoral," I mutter as he pushes inside farther and farther.

It's so tight and hot at the same time. I've never experienced anything like this before.

"I don't care," he says, slowly thrusting his finger in and out of my ass. "I need every inch of your body. Every hole belongs to me."

I never imagined it would feel this good, this pleasurable.

I can barely keep my eyes straight as I try to focus on my clit while he slowly amps up the speed. I moan, and he releases the pressure on my neck, but the pressure between my legs and in my ass only grows tighter and tighter.

"Oh God …" I mutter, my face turning red from the way I'm looking at my own fingers thrumming my clit.

"Come for me."

That's it. That's what I needed.

His voice. His touch. His craving. Him.

All I'll ever need is him.

My body convulses against both our hands, and I struggle to even stand as the orgasm takes over my body. I feel my ass tightening around his finger, just as my clit thumps. All my muscles play along as I ride the waves to ecstasy. Even my eyes roll into the back of my head. That's how good it feels.

"My turn," he growls into my ear, and he shoves aside my fingers only to dive right into me while his other finger is still inside my ass.

I gasp when he enters my pussy, thrusting up and down with ease. I'm so wet and so eager that I'm practically leaning into him. Two fingers inside me at once feels so good I almost explode again.

"Fuck, I want to bury myself inside you," he groans as he plows into my pussy and ass with just his fingers.

And for some reason, I can't stop wondering what it would feel like to have his cock up there, too.

"Yes," I moan, completely delirious with need.

His eyes, which never left mine, suddenly turn animalistic with a hunger I've only ever seen while we were in that cell.

When he first laid eyes on me and decided to eat me up.

"Say you're *mine*."

I don't even have to think twice. "I'm yours."

***

BEAST

I don't wait another second before I rip down what's left of the pants I got her and pull down my own zipper to release my hard cock. My fingers slide out of her with ease, and I push up against her entrance and thrust inside her pussy, not spilling even one drop of her wetness.

After watching her fall apart like that, I couldn't hold myself back any longer. I need to have her, need her to know there is nothing on this earth I wouldn't do for her. I would go to hell and back and slaughter everyone in my path to save her. To make her mine and no one else's.

"You belong to me," I groan as I bury myself deep inside her.

She whimpers with a mixture of lust and fear, but an exciting kind of fear. The kind that begs for more but doesn't know how to.

And I'm more than willing to give her everything I have to give.

I pull out and thrust back in again, watching her face and eyes unravel in front of me.

"Look at me fucking you in the mirror," I say, bouncing her against me from the back while I hold her tits and throat. "Look at how beautiful you are with my cock shoved up your pussy."

"Oh God …" she moans as I relentlessly plow into her.

I'm mad, completely crazed just from the snug fit of her velvety pussy around my thick length. Even when I have her now, it'll never be enough. I want to claim her, own her, consume her very soul.

"Beautiful," I whisper into her ear, and I lick the rim of her neck.

I bury myself to the hilt inside her and watch her unravel before me.

"Fuck," she says through gritted teeth, barely able to keep her eyes open.

"Don't look away," I growl. "See how much I want you."

I want her to know there is no one else I would rather be with than her.

She's the one.

The one girl who saved my life.

The one girl I've been dreaming of since I was first captured.

The one girl I would hunt down the world for.

She is the beauty to my monstrosity, and I refuse to stop until she sees it herself.

"Now come from my cock alone," I whisper.

She gasps, and another moan exits her mouth before her pussy contracts with my shaft inside it. Her orgasmic waves pulsate through my dick, and my god, does it make me greedy.

"Good girl," I groan.

I bring her closer to my body, shoving in as far as I can, growling with pleasure into her ear while she holds on for dear life. Her tits bounce up and down in the mirror, her eyes barely able to focus on me, but I make sure she's not going anywhere as I thrust into her.

One. Two. Three.

Deep inside her, I release my seed in several spurts, filling her up to the brim.

When I'm finally satiated and pull out, lots of it dribbles out of her and onto the floor.

Her legs are almost crossed as her whole body begins to quiver. She can't stand anymore, so I lower her onto the floor.

"Don't waste a drop," I groan as I go to my knees in front of her, scoop up my cum, and shove it right back into her pussy again. Her legs are spread, and her face is flushed with heat as I thrust my fingers in and out, picking more up along the way.

Every thrust is another moan, and I am in love with the sound. So much so that I keep going, despite the fact that I've already cleaned the floor and sullied her. I need more of her moans. It'll never be enough.

"Beast, stop," she murmurs between ragged breaths. "I can't …"

"Give me more, beauty," I groan, adding another finger.

Her pupils dilate, but she still doesn't move a muscle as I thrust my fingers in deep and begin to gyrate my thumb across her swollen, aching clit. She's all red and flustered, but I don't give a fuck as I keep going like a mad beast drunk on lust.

The sound of her moans is all I'll ever live for. All I've ever fought for. And if someone ever tried to take that away from me, I would cut them open and split them in half.

"Oh God …" Aurora murmurs, tilting her head back against my shoulder again.

"That's it, watch me make you come now," I say, my eyes on her at all times as she slowly begins to unravel and pull away from who she used to be.

All she has to be now is mine.

No ifs. No buts.

No more voices in her head telling her otherwise.

This is what a beauty like her deserves; all the fucking orgasms in the world until she fucking begs me to stop.

"Beast, I'm …" she murmurs.

"Yes, give me every last fucking drop," I groan as she spills out onto my hand again.

She moans out loud, and her muscles spasm around my fingers again, dribbling out more cum, which I shove right back in again. Every last drop of my seed belongs with her.

And when it's all over, I bring my fingers to her lips. "Lick."

Her tongue dips out like I command it to.

A filthy smirk forms on my lips. "Don't we taste good together?"

A hesitant but playful smile forms on hers as a pretty blush colors her cheeks. "Please …" she mutters, gazing up at me through the mirror.

She doesn't have to say another word. Just this one is enough to make me yield.

I pick her up from the floor and carry her to the bed, where I lie down with her in my arms. I pull her close to my chest and wrap my arm around her waist, cocooning her in my warmth.

I'm not only here to make her feel good.

I'm here to make her feel protected, too.

Because that's what a man does when he is deeply, madly in love.

Nineteen

Aurora

While Beast continues to snore loudly, I gaze at myself in the mirror at the girl I've become.

She's not at all like the girl I was months ago, when I still lived with my father, still played that piano with those gloves, still hid inside that mansion because I thought the world wouldn't want to see me.

But now … now I feel like I'm finally seeing the real me I was meant to be.

I can't stop looking at my body, my scars, my hands.

I used to see so much ugliness in myself, but now all I see is beauty. Just like he calls me.

And his unconditional love has shown me I'm so much

more than just the monster my father made me out to be.

And with a smile on my face, I touch my own skin and all the scars on my fingers and hands with love. All the love I've missed all these years when I denied myself just because of what one person taught me.

My father's opinion of me doesn't define me.

I do.

***

BEAST

When I wake up and miss her scent, I immediately sit up and look around. The sun is shining brightly, which means I've slept through the night. But she's nowhere in the room, and my heart rate instantly shoots up.

My woman is gone.

I jump out of bed and throw everything aside as I march out the door, not giving a shit about anything in my way.

I have to find her. What if she got taken?

Rage fuels my steps as adrenaline takes hold, but I come to an abrupt stop in the middle of the living room when I see her bent over to reach for something in the back of a cupboard in the kitchen.

"What are you doing?"

BONK!

"Ow," she murmurs, rubbing her head after she hit it against the cupboard. "Geez, you scared me."

"Sorry," I say. "I thought you were …"

"Gone?" She raises a brow at me, then gives me this quirky smile she's rarely sported, and I have to admit it makes me feel like grabbing her and throwing her over my shoulder. "You can't get rid of me that easily."

I smirk. "I meant by Lex's goons."

She makes a face. "Ah, so that's why you ran out of bed in panic."

"I was not panicking," I retort, frowning.

"Is that why you came storming out of the room?" she muses, placing a bag of rice on the counter. "And here I was thinking I was quiet enough so you could sleep."

"I didn't hear any sound," I say, stepping close enough until I can wrap my arm around her waist and pull her in like a fish being reeled in on a hook. "I smelled your absence."

"You sniffed for me?" She giggles.

I lean in and grab a fistful of her hair, bringing it to my nostrils and groaning with delight. "You know what your scent does to me."

She giggles some more when my grip on her waist tightens, and my cock begins to grow in my pants from her response. God, I fucking love this woman of mine.

"So what were you doing in here?" I ask.

"Trying to find some food, but this is all that's left," she says, pointing at an old bag of rice.

"We'll figure something out," I say, planting a kiss on

her cheek.

The last time we had this conversation, it didn't end well.

"We don't have any money. No jobs. No more family either," she says, rolling her eyes. "Not to mention the fact that we're still being hunted by Lex. My father." She shivers. "I don't think it'll ever stop. Or that we'll ever be safe."

I grab her arms and make her look at me. "I will keep you safe."

Her cheeks turn red, but her blush is accompanied by a look of worry. "But that's just it. It forces you to stay vigilant. To fight. And I wanted you to have a chance at a normal life."

My brow furrows. I never actually thought about it.

"I don't just want you as a beast. I want the real you too," she says, placing her hand on my chest.

I shake my head. "That's impossible as long as they live."

She averts her eyes, mulling it over.

I know she wants a life in peace, but such a thing is simply impossible in my world.

"What can we do?" she says, sighing. "I mean, if my father came back here, what's to say Lex and his guards won't find this house too?"

Her father. That sly bastard will put everything I fought so hard for in jeopardy.

My fist tightens, and I step away from her to grab a shirt from the closet.

She's right. If I'm going to protect her, I need to be proactive.

Get ahead of them before they make their plans.

"What are you doing?" Aurora asks as I put it on.

"I'm gonna check something out," I reply, marching out the door.

"Wait, where?" she asks.

"It's safer if you don't know."

I don't want her to worry.

"Will you come back?"

Her words make me turn to face her. "Always."

The smile that follows is all I'll ever need to bring me back to her.

And I hop into the car and drive off.

***

Hours later

I drive all the way back to the one place I've dreaded going back to. But I have no other choice. I need to keep an eye out on those bastards to know if my suspicions are true.

With a heavy heart, I drive up to the side of the house, wearing a cap I stole from a local store. If I'm lucky, the guards won't notice me squatting outside the house. At least not while they're this busy with an unexpected guest.

I peer through the front window as a van travels up the mansion's driveway. Out pour several guards, along with a man whose hands are tied behind his back and his mouth stuffed with a cloth.

They shove him inside and quickly shut the door, so I gaze through the other window and watch the scene in the living room unfold from the car. Lex doesn't even bother shutting his blinds before the guards barge inside with none other than Aurora's father.

I knew that fucker would get himself caught.

My muscles tighten. If I'd just taken care of him myself, he wouldn't be there running his mouth.

Lex yells at his men. I can't tell what he's saying, but I know he's pissed, judging from the protruding vessels on his face and his obscene gestures.

He grabs a tissue from his pocket and coughs inside. There's more blood.

The man is deathly sick, and still, he chooses to destroy everything in his path.

Aurora's father is pushed forward on his knees.

A gun is pulled.

My pulse quickens, and I stare without blinking.

Lex flicks his fingers at a guard who runs off to fetch some papers and a pen … then hands it to Blom, who begins to write something down.

My eyes widen when I spot him drawing some kind of map.

Fuck.
I knew it.
He's leading Lex straight to us.

I push the gear into reverse and hit the gas, not waiting another second before I spin around and drive straight back to the beach house.

I have to warn her.

I have to get her out of there before they come.

Driving as fast as I possibly can, I skid through the streets, ignoring traffic lights as I make my way across the city, back to the only person I've ever cared about.

She's not safe at that beach house anymore. Not now that her father's talked.

We'll have to find some other place to stay. Maybe one of my old hideouts from back when I was still roaming the streets.

Then again, it may be best to escape the city entirely.

Grumbling to myself, I race through the streets, my heart still far from calm as I finally arrive at the beach house. I park the car sideways and with screeching tires, not waiting a second before I jump out the door and storm inside.

"Aurora!" I roar.

"What?" she yells back from the bedroom.

The sound of her voice is soothing.

She's still safe. Good.

"What's wrong?" she asks as she steps out of the room. "What were you doing out there?"

"We have to pack now," I say as I walk past her and head into the bedroom, throwing every bit of clothing we have into the big suitcase inside the closet.

She follows me around. "Why? What happened?"

"Your father's been captured."

Her eyes widen, a horrifying look settling on her face.

But the worst is yet to come.

"Lex?" she mumbles.

I nod. "And he's going to tell him where we are."

Her pupils dilate too, and her face goes as pale as snow. "No …"

"They're coming."

She keeps shaking her head. "No, Papa wouldn't do that."

"He already did," I say, grabbing her arms. "I saw him draw up a map. He's pinpointing our location."

She sucks in a breath as though there's no more oxygen in the air. "You *saw*? You went back there?"

I nod.

"But why?"

"Because I knew I couldn't trust him," I reply.

She frowns. "Are you sure?"

I clutch her arms. "I saw it with my own eyes."

Her eyes tear up and fill with a kind of terror that haunts me. "Papa …"

"He is not your papa anymore," I say with a stern voice. "He never was."

"But he—"

"You have to let him go."

"What?" she mutters.

"We have to escape. Now."

She jerks herself free from my grip. "You want me to

leave him there to die?"

"He doesn't care about you," I say. "He gave away our location."

"What if he was forced?" She's trying to find reasons that don't exist.

He's soiled her mind so badly that she can't believe he would ever harm her.

So I grab her by the arms and make her look at me. "He betrayed you."

Her eyes grow even more watery. "But I can't just leave him there. They'll torture and kill him."

"You have to," I reply.

"But what does that make me? If I leave him there, I'm just as terrible as he is," she says, tears rolling down her cheeks. "We have to save him."

I frown. "No."

I pack the rest of the bags.

"We should at least try," she says.

"I already saved his life once," I bark back. "And it almost cost me my life."

She merely stares at me with disdain as I finish packing.

"Your father chose his own fate when he left this house," I add. "This is on him."

She growls, "But he is still my family. And you don't know if he was forced or not."

I've never seen her this upset before.

I may not understand much about family or love, but I was right when I called it a weakness.

"We have no time for this," I say, as I rush toward the car.

"Beast!" she yells, following me. "I am not abandoning anyone!"

I throw the bags in the back of the car and start the engine. "Now hop in."

"No," she retorts. "If he was forced, I have to save him. I can't just leave him there to die."

I stare at her through the mirror. She looks blinded by rage. And it's as though I'm looking at myself in the past.

"Get. In," I say with a deadly tone.

I'm not warning her again.

She folds her arms. "You're trying to kill the only family I have left."

"Aurora …" I say through gritted teeth.

"No. You don't want to take responsibility, but none of this would have happened if you hadn't come to my house to kill him."

There it is.

The one dagger she managed to find.

Driven like a stake right through the heart.

I burst out into a fiery rage. "You came to my house first with your father and killed my parents!"

Her eyes widen, and her lips part, but there are no more words.

All of them have been stolen by a single statement.

One I regret instantly.

But the damage is done already.

"You want to stay? Fine," I bark, overcome by my anger taking control as I hit the gas. "Don't fucking move an inch."

And without saying another word, I drive off.

Twenty

Aurora

When the car disappears from view, I stumble back inside. But as the door closes behind me, I sink to the floor, crying my eyes out as I curl up into a ball.

I never thought anything could hurt more than watching my own father get tortured, but I was wrong.

I was so wrong.

I cry out all the tears I've kept buried all these years. Tears for my mother, tears for the pain my father caused, and tears for Beast, who ripped out my heart and crushed it with his bare hands.

And for a while, I just lie there, trying to make sense of

this dread in my heart, wondering if I'll ever see him again.

I know what I asked would be an impossible task, but to not even try feels like something Lex or my father would do. Something only a monster would think of. And I don't want to be that kind of monster.

Even if my father betrayed our location, who knows what they did to him to make him give it away. He can't have stumbled back into Lex's hands … right?

My eyes open wide.

Lex.

His men are coming for me now. Who knows when they'll be here, but it'll be soon.

I push myself off the floor and look around.

I have to find something to defend myself. Put on something strong, something thick that can resist a bullet. But Beast packed all my clothes, so all I have left is a cutting board I found in the kitchen and a piece of rope used to tie the curtains.

I fish the same big butcher's knife my father used on Beast from the kitchen and tuck it into my pocket.

It's not much, but it'll have to do. I'll have to put my fears and worries aside and focus on trying to get myself to safety. Because if I know anything about Lex, it's that he won't stop until he finds me.

Even if I run now, he'll probably still be on my tail.

And this time … I won't have Beast to protect me.

***

BEAST

I rush to the nearest store I can find that sells knives and stuff a few in my pocket, then bolt off. The alarm goes off, but by the time the owner runs out of the shop yelling his ass off, I'm already long gone.

I do the same in a different shop that sells building supplies like big chunks of rope. I swoop it all up and tuck it into a bag I kept empty, then run like hell to my car and drive off without paying.

I head into a store that sells groceries and take only the food and drinks I need, stuffing it all into another bag when no one is watching, then head out again.

The cops must have been called numerous times already, but I don't care. I don't have a home, and I go wherever I need to go. They won't find me. I put on my cap and avoided all the cameras, which were easy to spot.

Even if they capture me on tape, finding me will be impossible, as no one will recognize me from anywhere. I haven't been in the system since I was a little boy. I'm like a ghost that never existed.

A monster trained only to kill.

And I don't steal without purpose or for money.

I steal to prepare.

When I have everything I need, I hop back into the car and race right back to the beach house. Adrenaline courses through my veins as I ignore the traffic lights and go as fast as I can, hoping, praying she's still there.

Since the minute I left, I've been wrecked by nothing but guilt.

Not a moment has gone by when I didn't wish I could take back the words I said.

But it's too late now.

My words are floating through her head, and when I spoke them out loud, I became the kind of monster I swore I'd never be.

***

Aurora

Screech.

Even a tiny sound puts me on edge.

I inch toward the window and push aside the curtain.

There's a car parked right outside. But it's not the one Beast left in.

Oh God. They're here.

Panicked, I close the fabric and step away from the windows. Sweat drops roll down my forehead as I walk backward into the bedroom and lock the door, even though I know it will never stop them from reaching me.

Nothing ever will.

Not without him.

Oh God, where is he?

Please, Beast, come back.

I grab my weapon, the knife, and hide underneath the bed. It's cold and musty down here, but it's the best place I could think of while my mind is going crazy.

I should've gone with Beast when I had the chance.

I don't want to end up in Lex's claws.

Not again.

He'll force me to go back into that cell, into the never-ending darkness, used only for his abominable, disgusting needs.

The thought of that wretched man putting his hands on me makes bile rise in my throat, but I swallow it back down.

BANG!

I jolt up and down from the noise of wood. That sounded like … the front door.

And it was definitely opened with violence.

Feet stomp all over the house. Not just two of them but multiple.

Adrenaline courses through my veins as things get pushed and shoved and thrown across the house. Every sound makes my eyes flicker and my heart rate shoot through the roof.

BAM!

Someone slams the bedroom door.

I have to slam my mouth shut to stop the squeal from

escaping.

Oh God. Will they see me?

Can I fight them off with this knife?

My fingers dig into the handle of the knife as I prepare myself for the worst of the worst.

BANG!

The door falls to the ground as though it was made of mere paper. Two feet appear from the rubble, and a man slowly walks inside.

I hold my breath and stare at the boots as they walk by the bed and circle around the room. My hand is shaking, and I physically have to hold it steady.

Until the man leans over the bed … and stares right at me.

WHACK!

I stab my knife straight into his foot out of pure instinct.

The man yelps in pain. "FUCK! She stabbed me!"

More men pour inside.

"She's under there!"

Shrieking, I fish the knife from his foot and slice around at their hands, desperate to escape my attackers. But there are too many, and soon one of them circles behind me and grabs my feet.

"No!" I scream.

He drags me out from underneath and flips me over on my back. I fight him off with the knife, cutting and slicing away as hard as I can, just like Beast would have done.

I slice right through his hand and cheek.

He roars in pain.

"Fuck, help!" the man growls at the others.

His hands are still on me, despite the blood dripping down his face.

"No, let go of me!" I scream, but the man quickly grabs my wrist and knocks the knife from my hand.

Another one kicks the knife away as the one who holds me sits down on top of me to grab my other wrist too, but I won't go down without a fight. I scratch away as hard as I can, clawing at his throat, leaving marks left and right.

"Get away from me!" I shriek. "Beast, help!"

The guy grabs a fistful of my hair and slams my head down onto the floor so hard everything begins to spin. "Where is he?"

"I don't know!"

"LIES!" the man growls at me, and he punches me so hard I can't see straight anymore.

He quickly straps my wrists together with a tie wrap and gets off me.

"Bring her back to the car. We'll come back for him later."

"No … no …" I mutter, still dazed.

When they drag me through the house, I bite down on the floor.

That's how desperate I am to stop them.

But even my teeth aren't strong enough to hold on.
WHACK!

A sudden hard kick to the gut has me groaning in pain.

"Don't resist, or I'll fucking cut you instead," the guard barks.

Blood drips all over the floor from my gums that sank into the wood as I desperately tried to cling on to the freedom I finally had.

But the pain doesn't faze me …

Not compared to the thought of the place I'm headed.

Hell.

***

BEAST

I swallow back the remorse and focus on driving to the beach house safely, but every passing second is another one wasted.

"C'mon, c'mon, c'mon!" I yell as I slam the steering wheel.

I push the car to the limit, slamming the gas as hard as I can.

When I finally get there, I park the car sideways, not giving a shit about etiquette. But when I jump out of the vehicle, my stomach drops.

The front door has been pulled out of its hinges.

A trail of glass and blood drops is scattered out onto the pavement.

I have never known true terror until today.

I bolt inside, almost tripping over my own feet. "Aurora?!"

My voice is strangled, and the more I call out, the more desperate it becomes.

"AURORA!"

My calls are returned with silence.

All that's left are shattered windows, broken down doors, a sharp, teeth-like indent in the floor, and a tiny trail of blood.

I go to my knees and dip my finger inside the trail, then take a lick.

The taste brings my blood to a boil. My muscles tighten against the fabric so violently it tears under the strain. My teeth grind so wildly against each other that tiny chips fly off.

I thought I knew what rage was. Until now.

Until Lex dared to take my woman from me.

But I will make them pay in fucking blood and bones.

Twenty-One

Aurora

I kick and scream and dig my heels into the ground as I'm dragged back to the one place I wanted to escape. But I would rather die than stop resisting their attempt to subdue me. I'm done playing the weak victim. I am not going to go quietly anymore.

"Let me go, assholes!" I yell, stomping down on the back of the man carrying me so hard he starts to wobble on his feet.

"Couldn't you tie her up better, dude?" he asks his fellow guard.

"Stop ignoring me!" I screech, and I bite down on the zip ties around my wrist in an attempt to break them.

"Help me carry her," the guy holding me says.

I kick him in the belly again, and he makes an *oompf* sound.

Suddenly, two hands lift my ankles up in the air, while the guy holding me pulls me off his shoulder and grabs my wrists instead, holding me like a piece of wood being thrown on the fire.

When the door of the mansion comes into view, I panic. "No, no, no!"

"Shut the fuck up," the guard growls as he kicks it open and hoists me inside.

I fling around inside their grips but to no avail. I can't win two against one.

WHACK!

A sudden hard hit on the floor in the middle of the living room makes me cry out in pain.

They threw me down like a piece of garbage.

The guard swiftly cuts through the zip ties that bind my wrists and marches off, shutting the door behind him.

Groaning, I come to a rise, but the fogginess in my brain instantly clears the moment I spot my own father sitting in a chair right beside Lex.

My stomach drops.

"Welcome back, dear," Lex muses, smiling like a crazed maniac.

But I can only stare at my father, who looks down at me with disdain.

"Papa …?" I mutter in disbelief that he's actually here

without fighting even a single second.

"You look like you've seen a ghost," Lex says, tapping his fingers against the chair. "Yes, Aurora, your father is here as well. Astute observation."

Tears well up in my eyes as I gaze at my father's, whose soulless eyes make me feel numb to the core.

He's calm. Far too calm.

Like he's actually here, willingly.

"You … You sold us out, didn't you?" I mutter.

Father doesn't even blink.

Beast was right.

He gave Lex the location of the beach house. But why? Did he want Beast to get captured that badly?

But he knew I was there too.

Why would he do this to me?

"You knew I was there too, not just Beast. You knew they'd come take me," I rasp, barely able to speak through my anger. "Why?"

His face tightens, darkens, and his muscles stiffen as he shifts in the chair.

Still, there's no response.

Oh God no.

This can't be happening.

Panicked, I push myself backward across the floor while Lex begins to laugh.

"Where do you think you're going?"

I bump into the door and crawl onto my knees to stand, but no matter how many times I jerk the handle, it refuses to open.

"Open this damn door!" I yell, punching the wood.

I know it's no use, but I've got to do something. Anything.

"C'mon, stop that bullshit and just sit down," Lex barks.

I turn to look around, but there is literally nothing in this room I could use as a weapon. It's like everything has been stripped in a premeditated fashion. Like they knew I'd be coming and that I would make trouble.

Lex points at the couch. "Let's have a chat."

I stare at him and my father, wondering what they've been scheming. Whatever their plans are, they can't be good.

"No," I growl from my corner.

Lex raises a brow. "Would you prefer it if I put you in the cell immediately?"

Panic seeps into my bones.

I swiftly spur into action and huddle to the couch, farthest away from both of them.

"Good girl." He looks over at my father. "See, a little motivation is all she needs."

"Hmm …" my father grumbles in response.

"Why? Why would you do this?" I ask him.

But there is no answer. Of course.

"Were you forced?"

Lex begins to laugh. "Nonsense. He came to me out of his own free will."

My eyes widen.

Beast … he was right all along, and I didn't believe him

because I stupidly believed my father still had a semblance of a heart.

"Where else was he supposed to go? He has nothing left," Lex says, laughing his head off like it's all one big funny joke to him. "He's lucky I didn't murder him on sight."

I swallow away the nerves when Lex picks up a cigar and lights it on fire. "I would've burned out his eyes if he hadn't told me the code to that fantastic bank account."

"So you gave him the money after all," I mutter. "You had it. Even before, when you were still free, you could've given it to him and set me free." I clench my teeth. Every last inch of guilt I felt over not trying to save my father vanishes. "You chose to let me be a prisoner here."

"Aurora … Did you honestly think your father loved you?" Lex muses, snorting. "Come now, he gave you away like it came easy to him."

"It wasn't easy," he suddenly interjects. "But your choices made it impossible for me to stand by you."

"What?" I frown.

"You chose that *beast* over me," he hisses, frothing at the mouth. "Your own father!"

"He saved your life!" I yell back. "And mine!"

"And where did that get you both?" Lex interrupts. "Right back into my arms with nothing left to offer." He takes a deep whiff of the cigar and blows out a breath in my direction.

"Was it worth it?" I growl at my father. "Trading your

own daughter for your life?"

He slams his mouth shut, too proud to even admit what he's doing is the lowest of lows.

"And I used to think you loved me," I murmur through gritted teeth.

"Love is overrated," Lex says, taking another whiff. "My Beast showed me that much."

Now he's got my attention.

"Oh, you thought I'd be content with just you? No girl," Lex says, tilting his head. "I won't rest until I have my dog back as well. Because what is a dog without its master? Nothing."

The way he talks about Beast is horrendous.

Infuriating.

And it pushes me beyond my limit as I bolt up, grab the box of cigars, and throw it right at him.

He catches it mere inches away from his face.

"Don't talk about him like that! He deserves to be free!" I yell in anger. "You're disgusting."

Lex shakes his head and puts the box back on the table, staring at me.

"Call me whatever you want, girl. It doesn't change the fact that he disobeyed my orders, and I am the one who's going to punish him for it."

The smug look on his face makes bile rise in my throat.

"But I have my money now ... and I don't need to take your lives if I can have something far more valuable," Lex continues. "Complete and utter humiliation."

He snaps his fingers, and guards pour into the room.

"No," I shriek as they grab ahold of me. "Don't!"

"Don't what?" Lex raises a brow. "Put you back where you belong?"

My throat clamps up, and it feels like I suddenly can't breathe anymore.

No, no, no!

I fight off the guard as he puts his hands on me, but I'm no match for two of them dragging me by the arms.

I have nothing, no power, nothing left to give except words.

So I throw everything I have out into the world.

Pain.

Pure pain.

"I never should've freed you from that chair!" I scream at my father, whose eyes are filled with bitterness. "I should've picked *him* over you and let you die!"

Lex blows out another breath laced with cigar smoke in my direction, wearing a filthy smile on his face. "Too late for regrets, girl ... down to the cellar you go."

***

BEAST

I race to the mansion in my car, not giving a shit about the speed limit. Every second is another one wasted. Another one she spends in his claws.

The mere thought of Lex even touching her with a single finger sends me into a maddening spiral of rage, and I roar out loud, slamming the steering wheel.

"Goddammit!"

I never should've left her behind like that.

Nothing in this world could ever be fast enough for me. I need to get to her *now*.

That blood on the floor was hers, and I'll be damned if I let him spill another drop of that precious liquid.

She's mine, and I don't fucking care what I have to do to save her. Even if I have to rip off each one of his guard's limbs or eat my way through them, I'll do it all for her.

When I finally get there, the tires screech as I slide the car sideways and peer through the living room window like before. There's no one there except for two guards, which tells me they just left the room.

But I know Lex, Blom, and Aurora are in there.

I can smell it.

Suddenly, someone knocks on the car window, and I turn my head in the direction of the sound, ready to bite some heads off.

But the face that appears momentarily catches me off guard.

"Hello," a dark-haired boy with a feather earring says.

Lex's son, Luca.

Twenty-Two

BEAST

I feel like I could spit fire. "What the—"

I ram open the door right up against him, shoving him down onto the ground. And I grab him by the collar and lean over to bark in his face. "How did you find me?"

"I just came back from my father and saw you chillin' in your car, and I thought I'd recognized you. Relax."

"Give me one good reason I shouldn't run you over right now," I say, grinding my teeth.

"Whoa, calm down, fucker," he says. "I'm not your fucking enemy."

My hold on his collar tightens. "Tell that to your fucking piece of shit of a father."

"Where'd you get that sudden rage from?" he spits back, glaring at my neck, which misses the collar. "And where the fuck is your collar?"

"Your father is not in control anymore," I growl back.

His eyes narrow and then open up like he's seen the light. "Oh … you've freed yourself. I'm surprised."

I grab him by the throat. The squeaky noises he makes are like music to my ears.

"Don't. I told you, I'm not your enemy."

"Why should I believe you?" I say through gritted teeth.

"I hate my father as much as you do," he says.

I lower my gaze at him, suspicious of anything this dude has to say. If he's anything like his father, I can't trust anything he says or does.

"I can help you get her back."

Now he's got my attention.

I lift him up from the ground and shove him against my car by the throat. "What do you know about her?"

"Nothing," he says. "Just that you want that girl my father's been obsessed about."

Obsessed?

Fuck.

So it's worse than I thought.

"What does he plan on doing with her?" I snarl.

"I don't fucking know," Luca replies. "But if you let me go, we can talk."

I let it sink in for a few seconds before I loosen my grip a bit. Not enough for him to escape, but enough for him to breathe.

He's Lex's son, and I would much rather use him as a bargaining chip, but he has far more inside intel than I'll ever attain on my own. He could be useful.

"What can you offer me that I don't have myself?" I ask.

"You have a plan?" he answers.

No, but I've never needed one.

"What do you think is gonna happen when you storm in there?" he adds. "They'll gun you down in a second."

"What do you suggest I do?" I retort.

"Come back to my place, and I'll help you figure it out."

I snort, but the guy looks dead serious. "That takes balls."

"Can show them if you want," he says, winking.

I wince in disgust and pull back.

Luca laughs. "Your loss."

He wrings free from my grip and pats down his shirt. "You almost damaged my best shirt."

"I'll damage your entire fucking face if you don't spill the details."

He holds up his hands. "Fine, fine. You don't have to get violent on me." He reaches for his pocket and fishes out a knife. "I can do that just fine myself."

I make a fist.

"Whoa, calm down, doggy boy. I don't want to use it against you," he says.

"Then why'd you pull it?"

"Self-protection." He frowns. "Do you think I like

getting manhandled?"

My nostrils flare. I still don't trust this fucker one bit, but I don't have many options right now, and he's the best one.

He toys with the knife like it's a game. "Look, I don't wanna fight you. I just want my father out of the way."

Okay. A son wanting to kill his own father? Interesting, though not surprising.

"Why?"

He shrugs. "Let's just say he's gone past his expiry date." He flicks the knife up and down as a smug grin forms on his face. "So what do you say? Are you up for it?"

I grimace. "Teaming up with you? No thanks."

"Oh, c'mon," he says as I sit back inside the car again. "I know a way inside."

I look up as he hovers over my door.

"I swear, it's not a trap," he says. "If it was, my father's men would've already been coming for your ass."

I grumble. "Lousy fucking trap if you ask me."

He snorts. "Hey, I wasn't the one playing detective outside someone's window twice in the same day." He flicks the knife around again like it's a goddamn toy, and I don't like it one bit.

A knife is a weapon, a tool to achieve a goal, murder. Specific. Effective. Nothing more, nothing less. But it almost seems like he enjoys the violent part a little too much.

"You could get yourself caught if you keep going like

this," he says.

"And what do you care?"

"I don't. But…" He suddenly opens the door to the back seat and jumps inside. "I do care what happens to my father."

I glare at him through the rearview mirror, wondering if this guy has a death wish.

"So if you wanna kill him, I'm your guy."

***

Trusting this sly fox was the worst decision ever.

I park the car at a diner and exit the vehicle.

"Why are we stopping?" he asks as he hops out too. "I thought we'd agreed to go to my place."

"Change of plans," I reply.

"What the fuck do you want to do here?" he asks, trailing me as I go inside the diner.

"Neutral grounds," I reply.

The server inside looks at us like she's seen the two worst-looking guys on the planet. Maybe it's the scars on my face … or the fact that Luca is still spinning that goddamn knife around like a shuriken.

We sit in a booth far away from the entrance, where no one will hear us.

"For a dog, you sure know your way around negotiating," Luca mocks.

"I'm not a dog," I reply.

He perches his hand underneath his jaw, casually leaning onto the table. "Then what do I call you?"

"Beast."

A smirk grows on his face again. "So you don't have a name? You just casually call yourself 'Beast'? That's what my father calls you, isn't it?"

"It's what *she* calls me," I reply.

He narrows his eyes, almost as if he's waiting for more, but I don't have anything to add.

"Weird." When I don't respond to this obvious taunt, he adds, "You're surprisingly short of answers."

Just because he's now suddenly interested in helping me doesn't mean I intend to be friendly.

"You wanted to negotiate. Now talk," I growl, almost ready to lunge at him across the table.

"All right, all right," he says, blowing off steam as he leans back. "I'm just saying, maybe we should get to know each other. Before we die fighting together."

"Together?" My lip twitches. "No fucking way."

"What, you wanna go in there all by yourself?" He snorts. "Way to get yourself killed in a second."

"I know how to kill," I retort, my hand turning into a fist just from the thought of getting my hands on Lex. "And I will fucking gut that son of a bitch and everyone on his side."

He laughs. "I like that attitude."

"You mentioned a side entrance," I say, cutting to the chase.

"Before I tell you all about that, I need to have some assurances."

"What do you want?" I ask in a low, monotone voice.

"His money and the house," he replies.

Of course. That's all this was ever about.

All of those fuckers are the same.

"Done."

"Well, that was easy." He snorts again.

"I don't care about any of that."

"What do you care about then?" he asks. "Revenge?"

"Aurora."

There's a moment of silence.

"You really want her that badly, huh?"

I don't answer. The look on my face speaks volumes.

"Every minute wasted here with you is another one stolen from her," I growl.

His brows rise. "And eloquent too. Charming."

I'm so done with this motherfucker. "Don't act like you know me."

"True, I don't," he says. "But I'd like to."

"Not a chance," I spit back. "This is a one-time thing only. I take her, and we disappear."

"Okay. Deal." He cracks his knuckles. "Anything else?"

"Her father. Fat blob, hairy chin. Don't touch him," I snarl. "He's mine."

"Fine. Don't care. Next."

"That's it."

"That's it?" he parrots.

I tilt my head at him.

"All right … well, that was easy." He flicks the knife again, almost like it gets him fired up. "I'm ready to beat the shit out of whoever needs some ass kicking."

Something about his eagerness to fight makes me wary. "Why do you want your father dead?"

"He hurt my wife," he replies, staring me dead in the eye. "And *no one* touches her."

I see.

So we aren't that different after all.

"Satisfied?" he asks.

I nod.

"I'll deal with your father," I say.

"Good. I'll provide backup."

"When this is all done," I say, shoving my finger so deep into the table that it bends, "I never want to see you, your family, or your guards ever again."

"Fine by me," he says, shrugging again like it's no big deal. "I already have most of his business. All I need is that final nail in the coffin." He clutches his knife firmly. "Then his empire is mine."

He fishes a small booklet from his pocket along with a pen and slams it down on the table. "Now let's get to the nitty-gritty part."

Twenty-Three

Aurora

I scream and pounce against the railing of the cell until my hands start to bleed. There is nothing to see, but I can feel the warm blood drip down my fingers. An awful reminder that there is still life among these concrete walls.

There is nothing I fear more than the darkness in solitude. Nothing ... except a door opening up at the top of the stairs.

A sliver of light streams through the crack.

I lean up to see with my mouth hanging open as though I'm catching the final drop of water from an empty hose with my tongue. But when Lex himself comes down the stairs, I push back and crawl into a tiny little corner.

"Hello, little monster," he muses, walking closer to the cage. "Enjoying your time-out?"

I don't respond. I have nothing to say that he hasn't already heard.

More guards pour down from the stairs, each one looking even more menacing than the one before. And something about the way they're looking at me makes my skin crawl.

Lex stares at me. "Are you going to come quietly?" His guards pull out their stun guns. "Or do we have to bring you by force?"

I swallow the lump in my throat and get up from the cold hard concrete floor. With my teeth clenched, I make my way to the door and wait until one of his guards has opened it.

"Good girl," Lex says through gritted teeth, and he flicks his fingers at his guards. "Take her upstairs."

Two guards grab me by the arms and haul me up the stairs. I don't fight, but I don't help them either. I'm terrified to get zapped, but at the same time, I refuse to make their jobs easy for them. This is my way of protesting. My only way of showing Lex what kind of a piece of shit he truly is.

They shove open the door, and the light blinds me so much I look away with narrowed eyes. But from the tiny slits, I still spot my father standing in the hallway, just looking at me with his hands in his pockets, as though it does nothing to him.

And it wrecks me. Completely and utterly wrecks me.

A father is supposed to protect his daughter from harm. And now he actively participates in it.

Tears well up in my eyes, but I refuse to let them fall for him.

The guard shoves me toward the stairs. "Up."

I do what he says but keep my eyes on my father for as long as possible, sending him the worst possible daggers with glares alone. I want him to know he did this. He is making me suffer. He deserves every ounce of guilt.

"Left door," Lex barks as he follows us up the stairs.

We go into the same room as before, the one with all the lavish furniture, the leather lounge, the thick red curtains, and the piano. His wife's room.

The guard shoves me inside and walks away, slamming the door shut.

I gulp down the lump in my throat.

On the bed is a woman in a thin, silvery-looking nightgown. She leans back on the bed, gazing at me with an interesting look on her face.

Sweat drops prick at my neck. "Who … Who are you?"

The woman looks at me with dead-fish eyes.

"Introduce yourself," Lex barks at the woman.

"Hello, dear. Don't think we've met before, have we?" the woman responds with a tentative smile. "I'm Anne. Lex's wife."

So she's back from her business trip. And she's not at all bothered by her husband taking hostages? Trying to murder people? Using me?

Or is he forcing her to accept his debauchery?

"You're not going to say hello?" she asks.

I just stare at her, blinking rapidly.

What is going on?

Why am I even here?

Suddenly the door opens up again and the guard steps inside … clutching my father's arm. "Get in."

My father and I glare at each other for a moment, and then it dawns on me.

My father bargained for his life with me … but how?

The guard pushes him down on a chair in the back of the room near the door and then ties his hands together behind it so he can't move.

Something is thrown on the floor in front of me.

A piece of fabric. If you can call it that. Because it's more holes than clothing.

Along with two gloves.

"Put that on," Lex commands. "Gloves too."

I gaze at the woman, but all she does is stare back nervously. Like she's afraid what might happen if I don't do what he says.

Slowly, the panic begins to rise.

I step backward until I bump into my father. When I glance over my shoulder, he says, "Aurora, put it on."

I shake my head. "What? You're in on this?"

Lex snorts. "I thought I wanted his head, but this … this is so much better than any amount of blood he could ever give me." He points at the outfit on the floor, a glimmer sparkling in his eyes. "Now put it on … and maybe, just maybe … I'll let you both live."

I shake my head, but the more I do, the darker his face becomes. So I glance at his wife, who should be reeling by now, but all she does is watch with a broad smile on her face like she's enthusiastic at the outcome.

And terror slowly begins to take over.

"Go on then … put it on," Lex growls.

The threatening way he stares at me makes me want to run, but I have nowhere to go. Nowhere to hide. No other choice but to do exactly as they say, or they will hurt me.

And I know they would because they've done it many times before.

Eventually, I lose all hope and lean over and grab the fabrics off the floor. My stomach drops as I hold the body piece up in front of my face. There are holes in all the important bits.

"Well?" Lex says through gritted teeth.

"Can I have a bit of privacy?" I ask, my voice fluctuating in tone.

He makes a face and then laughs. "Privacy? For wearing that?" But when he looks at his wife, he stops laughing and rolls his eyes. "Fine. In there." He points at the closet. The same closet I was in before when he made me wear his wife's dress.

With a heavy heart, I walk toward it, taking every second like it's going to be my last, stretching them to the limit.

But once the door closes, I cave in on myself.

"Beast," I quietly mutter to myself. "Where are you? I need you."

I know he can't hear me, but the words still flow off my lips like a whisper into the wind, a wish floating away into oblivion.

"What's the holdup?" Lex barks from the other end, knocking on the door. "Or do you want my guard to come inside and help you?"

"No, no," I mutter between unsteady breaths. "Almost done. I just need a minute."

"Hurry up," he adds with a stern voice.

The air is getting harder and harder to breathe in as I pull off my clothes one by one, dropping them all to the floor like a snake shedding its skin. I still manage to put on the outfit, despite all the drops of sweat rolling down my shivering body.

When I'm finally in the outfit, I fetch a bathrobe from the hangers and pull it over the skimpy parts so I don't feel so … naked.

Because that's all this is. A bunch of strings pulled together over my nude body.

The door opens, and a guard steps inside. "Come out. Now."

I nod at him through the mirror and turn around, walking as slowly as I possibly can to stretch out the time as much as possible.

But nothing can prepare me for stepping out of the closet straight into the lurid gazes of the people I hate so damn much.

Bile rises in my throat, but I swallow it back as I come face-to-face with my own damn father. "What's going on?" I mutter at Lex.

I thought my father would be long gone by the time I left this room, but he's still here, even though I'm dressed in the most inappropriate outfit. And Lex's wife is still here too. Both are watching me with ill intent.

Lex steps forward, an evil grin on his face as his hand rises to meet my face. "You know, I've always had this fantasy …" he muses, caressing my cheek with those cold, thick fingers of his. "For someone to share with my wife."

Tears well up in my eyes.

Please, no. Not that. Anything but that.

"So I'm going to give you one more chance to prove to me you're as willing as you said you were …" he says. "And I will make your father watch every inch of me corrupting you."

My father? Oh God.

When Lex attempts to remove the bathrobe, I shudder, and my stomach suddenly turns over. I run to the bathroom, sick to myself, and throw it all up into the toilet.

"That's no way to start and get me in the mood," Lex growls from the bedroom.

I quickly flush and get up, washing my face under the water.

You can do this, Aurora.
Just once, and he will set you free.

Ignore your father.
Ignore everything.

The sink slowly fills with water, and I look at the reflection of the girl leaning over. All I can think of is shoving my face inside until I no longer breathe.

BANG!

I lift my head and listen.

That sounded like … a bomb.

The same kind that was used when my house was blown to bits.

Another loud bang makes the house shake.

My heart stops.

Beast.

Twenty-Four

BEAST

Two minutes earlier

I open the trunk of the car and stare at the box filled with guns, knives, grenades, ammo, and more. Luca made me drive back to his building for it and stuffed it in the back, but this is the first time I'm looking at it.

I'm impressed.

"Where'd you get all of this?" I ask.

"Where do you think?" he retorts, winking. "Sons do what sons do best."

"Steal," I fill in.

"I prefer the term 'borrow,'" he replies, making a fake

rainbow with his hands.

"Thought I'd recognized these," I mutter as I pick up one of the guns.

"My father's preferred weapons," he says. "Hard to miss, but draws a lot of attention. He's dramatic, I tell you that."

"No drama, no attention," I growl.

He picks up a silencer and hands it to me. "This more your thing?"

I grab one of the smoke bombs from the bottom of the box. "No. This."

"Ahh … the stealthy type?" he muses.

"No," I say, and I grab some more of the pipe bombs he made. "I just like the element of surprise."

A taunting smile erupts on his face. "All right. I like the sound of that." He grabs a few guns, lots of ammo, and a couple of knives and tucks it all under his belt. "You ready beasty-boy?"

I grab as many weapons as I can before I close the trunk. "Don't call me that."

"You must be fun at parties," he says, as we both head in the direction of the mansion.

"What are parties?" I reply with the most stone-cold, dead-ass voice I can muster.

He stares at me from the corner of his eye while we approach the fence at the back of the house. "You really have been missing out."

I glance at him. "Why do you think I broke out?"

He grins. "Party-hard, fucker."

We both jump up and hop over the fence. Some alarms go off, but Luca snuffs them out with a quick bullet. Then we run to the back door, the one that leads into the kitchen, or so I've been told.

He made a whole fucking map of the house and included an attack plan, but if shit starts to fly, I'm throwing it out the window without a second thought.

The only thing that matters to me is saving her.

And if he dies while I'm in there trying to get my woman, it's his own fucking problem, not mine.

"Ready?" Luca asks.

I nod and chuck in a smoke bomb.

He knocks down the door with his foot when it explodes, and I go in first.

The room is filled with smoke, but I know how to make my way around the dark. With my gun held in front of me, I aim at anything that moves.

BANG!

One down.

Several of Lex's staff members flee the room, screaming in terror, but I gun them all down one by one. I do not care if they were guards or cooks. They worked for him, which means they hurt my woman and me.

BANG! BANG!

More go down like flies, but then gunshots finally erupt.

Luca is right behind me, shooting at the guards to my left while I focus on the way forward. I've imprinted the map he created onto my retina, going on pure instinct and memory as I walk.

"Code red, code red!" a guard yells into a walkie-talkie up ahead.

BANG!

I shoot him right in the head, and he collapses against the kitchen door, blood pouring from his wound.

Suddenly, there's a shriek. A familiar one. And it alerts all of my senses.

"Aurora," I mutter.

Every inch of self-control flies out the window as I storm toward the sound.

"Beast!" Luca calls behind me as he guns down anyone who approaches us from the left and the right. "Stick to the plan!"

"Fuck the plan, she's in danger!" I growl back, shooting back at someone gunning at us from the stairs.

When I'm out of ammo, I quickly shift to knives and chuck them at the men flocking around us from all sides. Some charge at me, and I slice through them like butter, cutting into their abdomens and gutting them in half with ease.

"You're gonna get us killed," Luca yells, trying to follow me.

"BEAST!" Aurora's voice calls me like a siren, drawing my attention upstairs.

She's in his room. Fuck.

The mere thought of that fucker putting his fingers on

her gets me possessed by the devil. Roaring out loud, I knife down anyone who dares to get in my way, stabbing guards in the neck and eyes until they squeal like the pigs they are.

I only turn my gaze to see where my backup is at.

"Go!" Luca growls at me, incensed that I'd ruin our plan of attack.

But there's too much at stake to take the controlled route.

Chaos is how I thrive.

As Luca offers me cover, I bolt toward the stairs, plucking the knives out of every single one of my victims.

There's another squeal upstairs, the sound going through marrow and bone.

And I roar out loud so everyone can hear, "No one touches my Aurora!"

***

Aurora

Present

He's here.

"What the fuck was that?" Lex growls from the room beyond.

But it feels like my body is firing up for something much more important than whatever destruction is happening downstairs. Beast's voice is all I need to inspire me.

I grab the towel hanging on the rack, tie it around my hand, and smash the mirror in front of me to bits. I grasp a thick shard and hold it tight. Two breaths in and out, and I storm toward the bedroom in a brazen effort to overpower my captors.

Anne screams when she sees me rush in. "Lex!"

I jab at him before he has a chance to react, thrusting the piece of mirror into his abdomen.

"You bitch!" he roars, swiftly pulling it out before smacking me in the face so hard I fall to the floor.

"Aurora, what the fuck are you doing?!" my father blasts through the room, but I ignore his yelling.

With bloodied lips, I crawl backward while Lex holds the shard like he intends to cut me with it.

"You dare to attack me in my own home?" Lex growls. "After the generous mercy I tried to offer you, one single day of pleasure with my wife and me… and you chose to hurt me instead?"

He clutches the shard so harshly his hand begins to bleed.

"I will make you pay for that," he hisses.

"No, get away from me." I crawl toward the window.

"Stop fighting him, Aurora!" my father barks from his chair. "This won't end well for either of us if you don't!"

"Listen to your father, girl."

I glance around to try to find anything else I can use to attack Lex. But all I can find is a clip that was used to tie up the curtains. I snatch it off the floor and hold it out in front of me like a weapon to keep him at bay.

Lex snorts. "What do you think you could do with that, girl?"

He laughs but then immediately groans in pain, clutching his side. The shard did enough damage to give me a sliver of time. And I use the opportunity to jump away from him across the floor, hurrying toward his wife. Without a second thought, I jump on the bed and hold the tiny trinket near her eye. "I don't want to do this, but you give me no choice."

Adrenaline courses through my veins, pulsating with violence as I watch Lex turn to seethe.

"Lex, help!" Anne murmurs, so I push the clip into her cheek.

"What the fuck are you doing?" Lex growls at me.

"Leave, or your wife loses her eye!" I yell back.

"What?" he scoffs, winching in pain.

"You heard me," I say.

"Aurora, stop this, right now!" my father blasts across the room, but he holds no power over me. Not anymore. He gave up that right the second he sold me out to Lex.

Lex laughs at me. "You think you're capable of violence?"

Maybe I wasn't before, but I've learned so much from my time with Beast. His fearlessness has left its mark on me. And sometimes we have to be our own savior.

"If I have to, I will," I retort.

"Lex! Please don't try anything!" Anne shrieks. "I don't want to lose my eye. It's not worth it."

"I don't fucking care!" Lex growls. "I won't let you threaten me, girl."

Oh my God, I can't believe it.

Is he really casting her safety aside? Just like that, like it means nothing to him?

I shove the metal into the skin right below her eye so deep it begins to bleed. Guilt fills my bones, but I stay put, clutching her tightly against me.

Until Lex storms right at me.

"You won't hurt her. You can't even hurt a fly," Lex growls.

Shit, shit, shit!

The second I attempt to stab her, he grabs ahold of my wrist and lifts it up into the air.

Too late.

"No!" I shriek as he knocks the metal clasp from my hand.

Anne jumps away from me, falling to the floor.

BANG!

Suddenly, the door is knocked in, and smoke erupts, filling the room instantly.

I cough and heave while Lex releases me. "What the—"

Guards burst into the room, shooting left and right at something beyond the door. My father and Anne begin to scream their lungs out.

"Code red, sir!" the guards bark at Lex.

"What?" Lex's eyes widen.

"BEAST!" I shriek, my body filling with vigor.

I know it's him. It has to be.

With a quick push, I shove Lex away from me and run for the bathroom door, but Anne grabs ahold of my foot, knocking me to the ground.

Oompf.

I look behind me and see her wretched hand wring around my ankle. "You're not going anywhere after what you just did," she says through gritted teeth.

I try to kick her away, but she's much stronger than I am.

BANG! BANG!

Gunshots fill the room, and I duck for cover underneath my own hands. Even though I know they won't protect me from the shots, at least they'll protect me from the cloud of dust.

Bodies drop to the floor. I can hear them smack like a sack of potatoes.

"AURORA!"

His voice makes me lift my head and hear his call.

A huge shadow fills the empty doorway, blocking the light, towering over us all.

And my heart almost jumps out of my chest.

He's really here.

More guards loom behind him, and my eyes widen. "Beast! Behind you!"

He doesn't even have to turn around. A quick swoosh

with his knife in a sideways fling slices through their bodies with ease, and he knocks them to the floor.

Lex pulls out his walkie-talkie. "I need backup! Wife's bedroom, now!"

BANG!

Beast shoots the walkie-talkie right out of his hand with a single gunshot.

Behind him, I hear more gunshots, the sounds making me hide underneath the beauty cabinet in the back.

"Help! Get me out of this chair!" My father screams his head off, but no one pays any attention to him.

Someone is still out there, shooting like crazy.

Is it a guard, or did Beast bring someone to help him out?

When our eyes finally connect, intense relief washes over me. "You're here."

"Of course I'm here," he growls back. "You're *mine* and no one else's."

His possessiveness always scared me a little, but now … now it makes my heart sing.

"So you've finally returned to me … Beast," Lex muses.

Beast's nostrils flare, and his lip twitches. "For your head."

But my eyes widen the moment Lex pulls out a gun and aims it right at Beast.

Twenty-Five

BEAST

BANG!

I lift my arm just in time to protect my face. The shot penetrates my forearm, but the pain doesn't faze me. I've been through worse, much worse.

Roaring, I pull out my own gun and roll to the side as I push in new ammo, then shoot at Lex from behind the bed.

The entire room fills with smoke and gunshots firing back and forth between us, half of them sifting through the walls. Blom is screeching his head off, and when I briefly throw a glance, he's chucked himself over in his chair and is now lying on his side. And not only that, he seems to have actually pissed his pants. Fucking coward.

"You think you can win this?" Lex roars when I need to reload. With a devilish grin, he rummages in his pocket and pulls out the same box that once made me cower in fear. A meaningless trinket now when he pushes the button, and nothing happens.

"What …?" he mutters.

I tilt my head and show him the scar.

His pupils dilate. "You … removed it …" His voice sounds like his heart; shriveled up and dead.

Lex's eyes turn to fire, and he shoots his gun all over the room, not caring who he hits. He's gone completely insane.

When his gun is finally empty, I lean over the bed and fire another time, then lunge at his wife and drag her with me to the bed.

"Let my wife go, you monster!" Lex roars, pulling out a new gun to shoot wildly, filling his own house with holes.

"Let Aurora go unharmed, and I will," I growl back.

"Fuck you, not a chance in hell," he retorts, firing again.

Aurora crawls across the floor toward me as I'm reloading my gun, but Lex suddenly lunges forward and grabs her by the ankle.

"No, no! Let me go!"

He's too quick to grab her, and before I can even react he's already grabbed her by the throat and lifted her into the air.

"No you fucking won't," he growls, pointing his gun at her temple, "My house is ruined because of you."

"I didn't choose any of this," Aurora tells him, her voice

crackling as he applies pressure.

"Let her go," I grit from behind the bed. "Or I swear to god, I'll—"

"You'll what? Sift her through with bullets?" A wicked smile forms on his face. Like he enjoys the idea of me having to kill her to get to him.

"Please …" Aurora mutters, terrified of the gun planted against her head. "Don't do this."

I hate—no, loathe—to hear her beg someone else.

The only one she should ever be begging is me.

"Do it, Beast. Try to kill me, I fucking dare you," Lex hisses. "At least it'll give me one last shot at some fucking fun for all of my wasted money and time."

I aim, clutching the gun so tightly the handle might break. But I know if I try to shoot now, I'll hit her instead. He wants me to risk it. He wants me to risk her life, but I refuse.

I can't lose her.

Slowly, I lower the gun.

He laughs. "You can't do it, can you?"

"I won't risk the life of the only person I've ever loved," I growl back.

"Love?" His eyes almost seem to glow with rage. "Love!?" The word itself seems to drive him mad. "All of my hard work—destroyed because of *love*!?"

"You're just like Blom," I sneer.

"Leave me out of this," Blom says, but I ignore him.

"You wouldn't know what love is, if it stared you in the

face," I add. I hold up his wife by the throat, making her look at him. "This is the man you chose. The man you fight for," I whisper into her ear. "He doesn't love you. He sees you as an asset. Something to use and discard."

She shudders in my grip, her eyes homing in on his.

"Don't listen to him, Anne!" Lex barks. "You know me. Better than he ever will."

"You didn't even care if I stabbed her eyes out," Aurora says, joining the conversation, even though she's still being held under shot.

"Shut it!" Lex growls at her, pushing the metal into her skin so deeply her pupils dilate.

She must be terrified—and it makes me want to squeeze the life out of the neck I'm clutching. But that would make me the monster he says I am.

"Beast, hurry up!" Luca's voice rings through the hallways.

"That's …" Lex's face turns white as snow. "You brought my son into this?"

"He brought himself into this," I growl back.

His eyes turn volatile, like an animal completely consumed by rabies. "You think I'll fucking let you win?!"

He shoots wildly at the door where several of his own guards are fighting with Luca, and he actually manages to kill one of his own guards.

"I'll fucking kill him myself for defying me!"

Suddenly, the woman in my arms grabs ahold of the gun in my hands and knocks it aside as she steals one of my knives from my pocket and leans to the side … only to chuck the knife straight at Lex's head.

Aurora shrieks as the knife bores a hole through his temple, blood trickling down his skull before he drops down to the floor, finally releasing her from his grip.

For a moment, everyone in the room stares at Anne, whose crazed eyes are filled with a hatred only a mother could know. "*No one* touches my son."

The most hated man in the room, killed by his own damn wife.

Well, that was an unexpected turn.

BANG!

The last guard drops dead in front of the door as Luca approaches. And he stands in the doorway, staring at both me, Aurora, and his own mother with an actual goddamn smirk on his face. "Sorry for being late. But not really."

Aurora stumbles away from Lex's body, and I immediately run to her to catch her in my arms.

"Oh my God, oh my God," she mutters. "I almost died."

"You're alive," I reply, patting down her hair. "You're safe."

"Thank you," she says, her voice breaking up. "Thank you for saving me. I thought you'd …" She can't even finish her sentence, but I know what she was about to say.

So I grab her shoulders and lower my eyes at her so she knows I'm serious. "I would scorch the entire fucking earth to rescue you."

Her cheeks flush and I grab her face and kiss her until both of us are out of breath.

"I'm sorry, I'm sorry for the things I said," I say between kissing her madly. "I'm sorry for leaving you all alone. When I came back with supplies, they'd already taken you."

"I'm sorry too," she says. "For what my father did, for what happened to your parents, your life, I—"

"Enough," I murmur. "None of it is your fault."

Every word is one too many. I know how she truly feels about me and what I feel for her.

The only thing pulling me away from her lips is Anne walking past us.

I watch as she kneels in front of her husband, or ex-husband, and pulls out the knife, then glares at me.

Is she planning something? Because it will only end badly for her if she tries.

She stands up and wipes the knife on her dress, then slowly makes her way toward me. "Let's end this bloodshed."

My eyes narrow. "I'm listening."

"Leave our family in peace, and we will do the same to you and yours," she says, glancing at Aurora. "I won't hold anything against you." Then she looks at me. "You are free."

It's the one sentence I always wanted to hear, but I always expected it to come from his mouth, not his wife's. A fitting fate for a man hell-bent on destroying everything in his path. Even the people he used to love.

"You have my word," she says, and she holds out the knife to me like it's some kind of fig leaf.

I take it and slip it back into my pocket. "The word of a De Vos means nothing."

"I have nothing left to give," she says, swallowing away her tears. "My husband is already dead, along with each one of his guards. You made sure of that."

The bitterness is hard to miss.

She takes a deep breath and briefly glances at her son. "But I'm willing to take my stride in defeat. As long as my son lives and thrives."

My nostrils flare. "Your son is a better man than your husband ever was."

Her face tightens. "I know." She licks her lips and looks at Aurora. "I'm sorry. I did not want any of this. But it was impossible to say no to him."

Aurora's still hiding in my arms, her body still shivering from the ordeal, but also because of the thin fabrics they made her wear. She nods softly, and Anne smiles gently.

"Killing my husband was the hardest thing I have ever done," she says, lifting her head. "But it was the right decision." She looks over at her son. "Something I should have done a long time ago."

Luca casually runs his bloodied fingers through his hair and strolls inside, tucking his gun back into his pocket. "Dad was done for anyway. Fucking cancer."

The bloodied coughs into the napkins ... that explains it.

"He tried to pull the company with him," Anne mutters

at her son. "But it's over now."

"Damn right it is," Luca says, as he marches over to his dad and actually plants a foot on top of his corpse. "You piece of shit just couldn't stop fucking with people, could you?" He kicks him a few times. "Even after I'd already taken most of your company, you just had to be a fucking asshole until your last. Fucking. Breath."

With every word, he adds another kick.

Damn, that guy really hates his father.

"Hello …?" A squeaky whisper from the corner of the room draws everyone's attention.

Blom's still stuck in that chair, covered in piss and gunpowder as he lies sideways on the floor.

"Help, please," he mutters even though all of us are looking at him like we want to roast him alive.

Luca snorts. "Yeah, no thanks."

"Luca, let's go. There are many things we need to arrange, like a cleanup crew and a funeral."

Luca glances at me. "I will honor the deal we made."

I nod at him.

"No!" Blom suddenly squeaks. "Not my money. My bank account."

My nostrils flare, and I march over to him and set him back down on the floor so I can look at him while I seethe with rage. "You're not keeping a dime of that money. Not a single fucking penny is yours." I point at Aurora. "She's the one who gets to decide."

Twenty-Six

Aurora

I clutch the bathrobe I stole closer and tie the knot around my waist so no one sees my breasts or pussy before I approach my father. He shivers in his seat, sweat drops rolling down his thick forehead.

He looks broken.

Just like I once did when I spent those nights in that cell, wondering if I'd ever see the light of day again.

"Please … Aurora … Help me out of here."

His begging does nothing for me. Not anymore. Not since he chose to rat out our position and sell me to save his life.

"You tried to get me to fuck him and his wife," I say,

grinding my teeth so hard I feel like I might break some. "Just to save your own skin."

Suddenly, a hand is planted on my shoulder. Beast leans over me, holding out his last gun. "I kept this last bullet … for you." He pushes it into the palm of my hand like it's his gift to me. Just like I once gave him the gift of hope in the form of a flower, he now gifts me revenge.

My body stiffens under the weight of the weapon.

And slowly but surely, I raise it to my father's forehead.

"No, no, please, don't do this," my father begs, his voice squeaky like a mouse.

Tiny. Insignificant.

Just as how he made me feel for all those years. All those years, locked up in his home like some princess in an ivory tower. All those years of subjugation and humiliation for the simple act of existing the way I am.

"Please, you're better than this, Aurora," he murmurs. "I love you."

"You don't know what love is," I hiss back, pulling off the safety. "I loved you with all my heart, and you broke me."

"I didn't mean to, but what else was I supposed to do? You would've never have been accepted by society," he mutters.

"*He* accepts me the way I am!" I scream, pointing at Beast.

My father looks defeated. It suits him well. "I only wanted to help."

"*Help?*" I parrot. My finger rests on the trigger, my mind reeling with all the suffering he's put me through. "You call forcing me to wear these gloves 'help'? You call giving me to the enemy like something to fuck 'help'?" Boiling with anger, I shake my head. "You sold me out and betrayed me!"

So this is how it feels. This is the kind of power that courses through Beast's veins.

I shove the gun farther into his head until the skin begins to ripple around the metal.

Years of misery I endured for this moment. This moment where I could punish him for all of the pain he inflicted on me out of his self-absorbed need to make me into something I never was.

He deserves it.

He deserves every inch of pain.

But to end it now would mean silence.

No more revenge.

No more suffering.

And that ... that's a fate too easy for him.

With a heavy sigh, I lower the gun.

Instead, I fish Beast's knife from his pocket and cut through the zip ties that keep him in that chair. Then I peel away the gloves Lex made me wear and chuck them in front of my father's feet. "I am beautiful," I say as I stare straight into his soul. "Despite everything you said and did to try to make me a monster like you."

He doesn't say a word.

"And I don't *ever* want to see you again, or I swear to God I *will* pull that trigger."

My father swallows.

Then I grab Beast's hand and walk. "Let's go."

"You didn't … kill him," he mutters. "You've got far more control than I do."

"Don't tempt me to go back," I say, tugging him along even though he walks slowly as though he can't believe I'm willing to let my father walk.

But I am not like my father.

I don't kill for money.

I don't kill for fun.

I don't kill for revenge.

I kill to protect.

And no one needs protecting from a squeaky, little, insignificant, powerless mouse.

Beast pauses, forcing me to stop, too, even though we're almost out the door. "Are you sure?"

"I don't want to be a murderer," I reply. "That's not who I am."

Beast brings his hand to my face, caressing me softly, reminding me of where I belong. "No … you were always better than him."

I smile.

Until my father laughs erratically. "Oh, I knew you wouldn't do it. That Beast puts thoughts in your head that don't belong there."

I try to ignore him. I really do.

Until he suddenly flies headfirst into one of the guards lying on the floor and grasps the gun in the man's hands … then aims it at Beast.

"You took *everything* from me!" he shrieks as Beast turns to look at him, unarmed.

I turn and shoot.

BANG!

The bullet enters my father's skull right between his eyes.

"No," I reply as he sinks down onto the floor, blood oozing from his head. "You did."

I march over to him to look into his eyes as his soul slowly begins to leave his body. "I hope you rot in hell."

When he breathes his last breath, I sigh along with him and let every bit of anxiety evaporate like snow before the sun.

"Damn girl," Luca says as he leans against the windowsill while his mother makes some calls to whatever people she knows to clean up the house. Or whatever is left of it. "I'm impressed."

I thought I'd be remorseful. Guilty. Sad. Upset.

But I feel … nothing.

Not even an inch of pain.

Beast's hand slowly snakes around my waist as I stare at my father's corpse. "Even when you gave him the opportunity to live out his life, he still chose to try to end mine."

"I couldn't let him," I say.

He pulls me in for a sideways hug. "I know, beauty. I know. You're a million times better than he could ever dream to be." I lean into him as he slowly pulls the gun from my fingers. "It's over."

I breathe a sigh of relief as he tucks his gun back into his pocket and laces his fingers through mine. "Let's go."

He strings me along until I have no more reason to stay. And we walk out the door and head downstairs, stepping over all the bodies of all the people Beast had to kill to get to me along the way.

And something about that is … humbling to the core.

Until Luca suddenly runs after us down the stairs. "Wait."

We pause and look over our shoulders at him as he clears his throat.

"Hey, I don't want to walk all over your obvious corpse parade, but do you even have a place to stay?" he asks.

My mind immediately goes back to the beach house and how violently torn up it must be, thanks to his father.

Beast pulls me along toward the front door.

"I can give you one of our vacation homes."

Now he pauses.

I turn to look at Luca again. "Why would you do that?" I ask, suspicious of his offer.

Beast tilts his head as though he's willing to hear him out, and I wonder what those two talked about and concocted that makes them so trusting of each other all of a sudden.

"Wait, how did you two even come together like this?" I mutter.

"Long story," Beast replies.

Luca smirks. "It was my father's time to go." He whistles and points at the window like he's literally pointing Lex's ghost the way out. "Anyway, the point is, if you need a place to stay, I can hook you up."

"What's the catch?" Beast asks, narrowing his eyes.

Luca shrugs. "None. I just don't want any more fucking trouble."

Beast merely glares at him like he's actually considering the option.

"Can we trust him?" I whisper at him.

"No. But we don't have anything else. The beach house is destroyed," he replies.

"There's only one key, and I can give it to you."

"Why?" I ask him.

"As a thank-you," Luca replies, stomping on the body again like he wants Lex to look disfigured. "For helping me end my father's legacy."

I swallow. This guy isn't someone you mess with.

But he's offering something that we don't have. Something we're desperately looking for.

A place to call home.

So I look at Beast, and he looks at me. "What do we have to lose?"

Beast mulls it over for a second. "No, thanks."

"Well, then at least take my father's stolen stuff back,"

Luca says, handing him some papers. "It's from Blom. I found it on the nightstand. I saw the bank account number and figured this is what you were talking about in the diner."

I gasp. "You actually made a deal at a diner with this dude?"

Luca smiles. "The fucker is smarter than he looks." He adds a wink.

"Hey," Beast growls.

Luca raises his hands. "Just messing with you. Like I do with everyone."

Beast's nostrils flare, but he doesn't respond further because he's too busy checking out the papers that carry my father's secret bank account details … along with all the codes we'd need to access it.

"I don't think my father got the time to use any of it, and neither did I, obviously," Luca says. "So consider our short team effort to be officially finished now. I'm gonna call some people. Get rid of all the bodies. Start fresh. You should too."

Luca runs back up the stairs to his mom, who is waiting for him while still talking on the phone.

I squeeze Beast's hand. "Are you sure about this?"

He nods. "I would much rather spend a million years fixing up the place we finally had to ourselves than spend one more second indebted to anyone." He squeezes my hand back. "Now, let's go home."

Twenty-Seven

Aurora

When we're back in the beach house, I look around and marvel at the mess that's left, completely dumbfounded by how we're supposed to clean this up. Most of the furniture is upturned and ripped. Vases are broken, and plates and knives are scattered all around. Things are upside down, the curtains are torn, and the floor is still stained with blood.

This is gonna take a while.

The door behind me closes, and I turn to look at Beast, who just stands there in the door opening, watching me.

But the way he looks at me is what makes my heart flutter.

So ... primal.

And it makes me step back.

Just an inch.

But it's enough to fan the flames behind his eyes.

"Stop," he growls.

I immediately listen. Not because I'm scared, but because I know what he wants. Me.

So much that I think he'd actually chase me and pin me down if I ran.

And that's the part that makes me gulp with excitement.

"But we've only just gotten back, the place is a mess, we need to clean it, and I'm still wearing this bathrobe and—"

One finger to the mouth is enough to silence me.

And I don't know how or why he can always make me quiet so easily.

It's as though he quells the storm raging in my head, calming the voices that tell me to be active, be productive, be helpful, just like my father taught me to be.

But my father is no longer here, and he has no more control over me.

Beast does.

Every breath he takes seems more ragged than the one before, his broad shoulders straining in his protective gear, which he slowly begins to take off. A loud thud is audible as each item drops to the floor, but I gasp when he actually drops his knives and guns too.

"But you take those with you everywhere," I mutter.

"I don't need them for what I'm going to do," he replies, his voice low, husky.

"What … what are you planning to do then?" I ask, my voice crackling from the mere thought of him lunging at me and devouring me just like he did when we were in that cell.

After getting rid of all his gear, he stalks toward me, wearing only a thin black shirt and a pair of army-green shorts. My heart is thumping in my throat by the time he's right in front of me. He easily towers over me and then some, blocking the view, preventing me from looking anywhere else but at him and his giant, bulky body that could easily sweep me off my feet or rip me apart.

And I swallow from the mere idea of him having his way with me like the aggressive, powerful beast I know he can be.

"I'm not going anywhere," he says.

"I know—"

"No, I don't think you do," he interjects. "I walked away last time when you needed me the most, and I almost lost you."

I stare at him, not knowing what to say.

"But I would kill every last man on this fucking earth to save you." He pauses, the weight of his words sinking in. "I will never, ever abandon you," he says. "Do you understand?"

I lick my lips and nod.

He tilts up my chin with a single finger. "I don't want anyone else but you."

It's as if he can see into my mind because when we were here together before, I always wondered when he'd want more. When he'd decide to just be free and do whatever he wanted. Explore the world. Kiss other girls.

It's his right. He's never had that kind of freedom.

Yet we're here now, together again, and he's telling me he only wants me.

And something about that is so incredibly humbling.

"But I don't want to hold you back, to be a bu—"

His finger lands on my lips. "No. Don't even think about saying it." He leans in. "You've never held me back. You gave me the freedom … to do this."

The bathrobe falls to the floor. Suddenly, his fingers curl around the racy outfit Lex made me wear, and he rips it to shreds with ease. I gasp in shock at how little effort it takes to tear it all away and leave nothing to the imagination.

"No one else gets to touch this body but me," he whispers, sliding his hand up my waist.

I blush, my heart still racing from his very touch. "Yes."

His fingers briefly skim my nipples, making me acutely aware of how much I want him to touch me and remind me I'm his and only his.

His lips are close to my ears as he whispers, "Say it. Say you're mine."

Why would he ask that?

Unless … he thinks there's even an option I wouldn't be.

"I'm yours," I whisper, feeling powerful that he'd even need me to say it.

His fingers clasp around my nipples, twisting until I gasp with surprise. "Good girl."

He grabs my three-fingered hand and brings it to his lips, planting a kiss so sweet I almost die. It's like he never once saw anything but …

"My beauty," he says.

Suddenly, he sinks down onto the floor onto his knees right in front of me. He kisses my belly, my thighs, my calves, all the way down to my feet. One by one, he showers them with kisses, making me feel so damn high on love that it's insane.

"What are you doing?" I mutter, completely confused by this sudden adoration at my feet.

"Apologizing, my way," he says, gazing into my eyes with complete and utter devotion. "For not showing you how much I love you."

Now my whole face heats up. "You don't have to—"

"Yes, I do," he says sternly. "You still don't believe you deserve me."

"I … I …" I don't even know what to say.

"Even when you're so willing to give yourself to me," he says. "You still don't think you deserve to be treated with love." He plants a kiss. "With grace." And another. "With passion."

Slowly the kisses begin to rise to my knee.

"All I've ever known is … not being worthy," I mutter.

"Your father was wrong," he says, gazing up at me with those soul-crushing eyes. "He called you a monster, but the only monster was him for making you believe that lie." He presses a kiss onto my knee and clutches my leg so I can't move. "All I've ever seen in you is beauty." His lips slowly drag up to my thighs. "It's not your skin that defines you but the size of your heart. Yours is the size of a mountain, and I want nothing more than to climb to the top and bask in your glory."

My eyes begin to grow watery.

All my life, I've been treated as less than others, even though I tried so hard to do my best. And it's as if finally someone is seeing me for who I truly am. For who I want to be.

And when he reaches the crevice between my thighs, he says, "So let me worship the fucking ground you walk on."

***

BEAST

I cover her pussy with my mouth, not giving a shit whether anyone can see us through the torn curtains. I need her to know I'm all hers, just as much as she is mine.

She is my scarred beauty, and I am her fucking beast unchained.

My tongue dips out to take a desperate lick, the taste as divine as I remember, tainted only by the memory of another trying to have what belongs to me.

But they paid the price, and now all that's left is to make

amends.

I will love my woman like she loved me. Give her everything I have and more.

"My freedom was worth nothing if I couldn't have you," I say between licking her sensitive pussy. "So let me take *everything* you have to offer."

It's all I'll ever need, all I'll ever want, and I'd rather die than not have her right this very second.

Her legs slowly widen as I push them apart so I can shove my full face between them and eat her out. I'm on my knees, lapping her up like there's no tomorrow, and I'm loving every second of it. Her body quakes, but I hold her steady, my fingers digging into her thighs as I kiss and suck her clit.

"Oh God," she murmurs, her body shivering with delight.

"Say my name." I press my tongue onto her clit and swipe. "Call me how you've always called me."

"Beast," she moans, and the mere sound alone instantly gets me hard as a rock.

That name was once a device to control me, to degrade me. But since it rolled off her tongue, it's given me nothing but power.

"I'm yours," I murmur, licking and sucking at her swollen clit. "And you are mine and only mine."

"Yes," she mewls with delight.

She starts to tiptoe on her feet, barely able to hold on, so I grab her hands and put them on my head. "Grab me and hold on because I'm not going to stop. Not until you've given me at least four orgasms."

"What?" she gasps.

I gaze up at her through my lashes while I continue to lick her pussy, wanting her to see every inch of me treasuring her body like the prize she is. "You heard me. Now give me the first."

Her whole face turns as red as a strawberry. "I can't. I don't know how."

"Yes, you can," I growl, and I slap her ass in response to her denial. "I won't take less. I need all of you. Now," I say, groaning against her pussy as I flick her clit. "Come."

Her moans go higher and higher until I suddenly feel the wetness gush from her pussy. I immediately stick my tongue inside and lap all of it up. The taste turns me on like crazy, my cock bouncing up and down, eager to bury inside to the hilt. Not fucking yet.

I grab her by the ass and lift her up while she squeals.

"What are you doing?" she mutters, still completely hazy from the orgasm.

I plant her down on the kitchen countertop and shove everything aside, not giving a shit that I'm creating more of a mess. Nothing is as important as showering her with all the love I have to offer. Just like she gave to me when I needed it the most.

I rip my shirt over my head and throw it aside. It'll only get wet anyway.

Then I grab the only stool that's not broken, sit in front

of her, and splay my hand on her belly, pushing her down. "Let. Me. Eat."

I groan as I lower myself between her legs and take what's mine, leaving no crumbs.

She moans and bucks against my mouth as I drive my tongue inside and circle around, feeling my way around until I've found the spot that makes her writhe. I apply pressure in all the right places, watching her twitch and listening to her moans for signs. Every breath is another one in the right direction until I can feel her muscles tighten inside her.

"That's it, beauty. Let me give you all the attention you deserve," I murmur, covering her pussy with my mouth while I thrust inside.

She moans louder and louder until another orgasmic wave makes her whole body tense up. The wave of wetness fills my mouth and runs down my chin, and I lick it all up because my woman's bliss is the best gratification a beast like me could ever fucking taste.

With a ragged breath, she leans up on her elbows, throwing me a ravenous look. She wraps her arms around my neck, inching closer as I rise to my feet. "I want to give it to you too."

"Not yet," I groan, despite wanting to very much.

This isn't about me or my needs. I can fucking wait an eternity if I have to as long as she is mine.

I grab her by the ass and lift her, carrying her to the bedroom, where I lie down ... with her perched on top of me. I push her forward until she's right above my face. Her body is covered with salty dew, and I lick her thighs, every lick better than the last.

"Sit," I groan, flicking my tongue back and forth, barely able to reach her clit.

Her eyes widen, her cheeks white as snow. "What—"

"You heard me. Sit on my face," I say.

"But I can't—"

"Yes, you can," I reply, gazing directly into her eyes as I push her thighs so hard she can't stop herself from lowering onto my mouth. "Now ride my face."

Her face goes from white to red with the snap of a finger as I slowly begin to wiggle her back and forth. My mouth is shoved into her pussy, and I lap her up like this is the last time I'll ever have to take a lick. My tongue pushes against her clit until it becomes swollen again, and she slowly begins to gyrate on top of me, unable to resist.

I know she loves the feeling as much as I do. And I want her to take control. I want her to be the one to satisfy herself. To feel powerful in her own body. To feel so fucking wanted she can't stop herself from taking all I have to give.

"God, you taste so fucking divine," I murmur against her flesh, sucking and licking as hard as I can.

"It feels so wrong," she whispers.

"Wrong in your head …" I murmur, suckling at her clit. "Right in all the good places."

The more I lick, the more frantic she becomes, and when I push my tongue into her pussy, she moans out loud.

The sound is such a turn-on that my hand instinctively moves down to my pants, and I grab my rock-hard dick and begin to play with myself.

"Oh God, don't stop," she murmurs.

I pull my tongue out only to say, "Fuck my tongue like I fuck your pussy."

She bounces up and down against my mouth and rolls herself around my face, covering me with juices, the scent making me drunk on lust. Groaning, I pull out my dick and jerk off while she fucks my mouth like it belongs to her, and it fucking does.

I don't want this mouth on any other girl but her.

I've never wanted to have someone ride my tongue until today.

Until she reminded me of just how much I love her and just how far I'm willing to go for her.

To the end of the fucking earth and I still wouldn't give up.

"F-Fuck," she murmurs.

I don't hear her swear often, but I love the sound.

"Yes, come all over my mouth," I groan, circling my tongue inside her.

She clutches the headboard, desperate to hold something as her pussy clenches and all wetness pours out. Her moans sound strangled like she's almost out of breath. My eyes drag over her body, over the sweet, supple skin, her perky tits and peaked nipples, all the way to her scrunched-up face lost in blissful satisfaction.

And even though my cock is still brimming with unspent seed, I am more than fucking satisfied.

Because this … this is nothing short of perfection.

***

Aurora

I'm completely lost in euphoria, my whole body humming to the tune of the orgasm I just had. Nothing has ever felt this good. And even though the house is still a mess and we've done nothing to fix it, I don't even feel remotely guilty. Because he made me feel gorgeous. Wanted. Sexy.

His strangled groan makes me look down, breaking the orgasmic trance I felt I'd landed in. His eyes are narrowed, his body straining beneath me. And I quickly lift myself. "I'm sorry. I didn't mean to crush you."

He bites his lip and moans. "I *want* you to crush me."

A blush spreads on my cheeks, but it quickly fades when I realize his whole body is still tensing up. I follow his rigid muscles down from his shoulder, my gaze following his arm until I find his hand … clutching his pulled-out veiny, throbbing dick spewing pre-cum.

Oh God.

My orgasms push him so far into lust that he can barely contain himself. He pulled his dick out of his pants and started playing with himself while I rode him. He's on the brink yet still thinking of me and me alone.

So I slide off his face and down his body, dragging myself over his cock, even though his hand is still there.

"What are you doing?" he growls. "You still owe me one orgasm."

I lift myself and push the tip inside. "I want to do it together."

I've never been this bold, but I want to do this. I want to be brave. To feel fearless like him. So I sink down onto his length, watching every inch of his face unravel with pure ecstasy.

I slowly begin to ride him, pushing myself up and down his shaft while on my knees, barely able to sit on top of the thick slabs of thigh. But he props himself up and grabs ahold of my hands, entwining his fingers through mine. And when I look into his eyes and see the pride in them, I feel as fierce as a lioness claiming her beastly king.

"Fuck," he groans, his knees bucking, unable to stop himself from thrusting in. "Use me. Ride me. Own my fucking soul, Aurora."

No one has ever said those words to me, and they hold a kind of power akin to touching the sun.

His head tilts back, a labored moan emanating from deep within his throat, as though it's taking every ounce of him not to come right there and then.

"Don't hold back," I murmur, and I lift his hand to place it on my breast.

He squeezes my nipple and rolls it around between his

fingers until I moan out loud.

And when my eyes roll into the back of my head, I feel him spurt his cum deep inside me, roaring out loud. It's so much, I can feel it ooze out of me, but I don't care. My orgasm overtakes my very soul, my body shaking like I've arrived in heaven.

And when it finally subsides, I collapse on top of him, our fingers still entwined, bodies united.

His breaths are heavy but controlled, and I can hear him smell my hair, just like he used to when we were back in that cell. But all it does is make me smile.

"I love you, Aurora," he whispers after a while.

And you know what? I actually believe him.

Nothing can break the radiant smile on my face as I reply, "And I love you, Beast."

I'm lying on his naked, beastly body with all my scars and imperfections, feeling nothing but beautiful. Just as he says I am.

And I finally realized what I always wanted was right here, with him. This … this is all I'll ever need to feel loved … to feel home.

Epilogue

Aurora

Weeks later

"Hi, English please," I mutter as I place my stuff on the counter.

I push some money onto the counter and watch the cashier be confused. "This is way too much for a sandwich and a Coke."

"Oh, I know. I'm just paying it forward," I reply with an awkward smile.

The cashier's eyes narrow, but he still accepts the cash, like I'd hoped he would.

I won't tell him what it's for, but I know the real reason.

A long time ago, I promised myself I would pay back everyone I owed. And I'm starting here with this store where I once stole something when I was in dire need.

Now that I finally have the money, I want to do things right. And I'm going to use my father's money to do it as a big middle finger to him.

Because now I'm using his money for all the things he'd never once even think about.

"There you go," the cashier muses.

I take the food and leave more money scattered throughout the store before I make a dash.

Then I walk all the way back to the place I once stayed in the tiny alley. I don't use the car; I parked it on the driveway of the woman we stole it from while she wasn't home and walked back to use the bus instead. I'll buy another secondhand car later.

Dirk is sleeping in his corner, as usual, so I sneak closer and plant the food and drink beside him under his cardboard box, then place a whole wad of euros next to him.

After another smile, I walk away.

I don't need to see his reaction to be happy. He deserves so much more in this life than what I could give him, but it was all I had left on hand.

And maybe, just maybe, I'll return here later to see if he's finally flown free.

Back to the people he loves.

Back to a normal life, just like me.

***

The next day

I put the pot of paint aside and marveled at the floral design I had made on the wall. The paint wasn't cheap, but I've got money to spare now that I've gotten my father's account to my name. There is more than enough in that account to keep us happy and healthy for life.

But all the money in the world couldn't replace a haven like this. A haven we created by hand after cleaning and fixing up every inch of this house.

Beast is still hammering nails into the wood when I say, "I'm done!"

He pauses and lets go of his hammer, the nail still stuck between his teeth as he comes to the bedroom to gaze at what I created.

"I'm not good at it, but it's better than what it looked like," I say.

He spits out the nail and says, "Better? It's beautiful." He grabs my waist and pulls me close, pressing a kiss onto my temple. "Just like you."

"Stop," I say, laughing when his fingers begin to squeeze my flesh like he's attempting to tickle me.

"No, not until you admit that it's gorgeous," he replies, fingers digging into my skin.

"Okay, fine, it's gorgeous," I say. "I did my best."

"Exactly," he replies, licking his lips as he stares at the

flowers. After a while, he releases me and approaches the paint, touching the dried parts with his fingers like he's inspecting it up close.

"It … reminds me of that flower," he says. "Before it dried out."

I blush. "I actually based the design on that."

He turns to look and smiles. "I'm amazed you still remember what it looks like."

"Of course, they used to grow outside my father's house, remember?" I reply, tucking my hair behind my ear. "I just wanted to give this room a special meaning, just like that flower."

He approaches me and grabs my hands, raising his eyebrow at me. "And what kind of special meaning is that?"

"Hope," I say, rubbing my lips together. "And unconditional love."

"All the things you've given me," he says, wrapping my own arms around him as he stands in front of me. "And all the things I won't ever stop giving to you." He leans in and presses a damp, sultry kiss to my lips. "Beauty."

I laugh against his lips. "Why do you keep saying that?"

He doesn't often smile, but when he does, it's the best feeling in the world. "Because it's true."

"But you don't have to say it every day."

"Yes, I do. And I'll keep saying it until you believe it too," he retorts.

He tips my chin up and smashes his lips onto mine, reminding me of his unforgettable hold on my heart, only stopping for a breath.

I quickly push away and step back, licking my lips with excitement.

"Aurora …" Beast warns.

I know he hates it when I walk away from him.

Especially when he wants to claim me like that.

"I have a surprise," I say.

His brow furrows, and his eyes narrow. "I don't like surprises."

"I know you don't, but this is a good one," I say as I walk back out of the bedroom. "I promise." He follows me into the living room, and I go into the kitchen and huddle onto my knees so I can reach the small cabinet in the back.

And I pull out a small pot I bought and the seeds I kept hidden underneath. I stand and hold it out to him. "Ta-da."

He tilts his head like he's confused. "What is it?"

I smirk. "Take a guess."

"A pot," he replies stoically.

I hold up the seeds. "No—well, yes—but look." I shake the bag.

Only after a while do his eyes finally widen. "Is that … the same pink flower?"

And when I nod, his eyes begin to shine with a kind of radiance I've only ever seen once before … when he first gave that flower back to me, and he saw in my eyes that I remembered him.

***

BEAST

The moment I realize what she's holding, I grab her and collect her in my arms, lifting her off her feet as I hug her tight.

"Can't. Breathe," she mumbles, and I quickly set her down again. She pushes the pot into my hand.

"But why? And how?" I ask, frowning. "You didn't go back to your old house, did you? That place could still be dangerous."

The stern look on my face makes her stammer. "No, no, I just knew which plant it was so I bought some at a local florist."

"Good," I say. "Because I don't want you to go back by yourself." I grab her hand. "If you do ever want to go back, tell me."

She blinks a couple of times. "Why?"

"So I can come and protect you."

Her smile brings so much light to this house.

"Thank you," I say, clutching the pot tightly. "It means a lot." I hold it out to her and add, "Will you do the honors?"

She nods and opens the tiny bag, plucking out a single seed, then pushing it into the dirt. "Water it every day, and after a while, a beautiful flower will grow."

I put the pot on the kitchen counter.

"You don't like it?" she asks.

I turn to cup her face and caress her cheeks. "Why do you always keep doubting?"

"Because … I'm always afraid you …"

"Will leave?" I fill in.

She blushes. "Won't be happy."

I tuck her hairs behind her ears and make sure she looks at me. "Aurora." I fish the dried-up flower from my pocket. "I kept this … for years. Do you know why?" I pause so she understands I'm serious. "Because I told myself that one day I would find the one who gave this to me."

Her eyes tear up along with a gorgeous smile forming on her face.

"You are mine. I do not let go of what's mine." And I bring her lips to mine and seal my promise with a kiss. "Ever."

THANK YOU

FOR READING!

Thank you so much for reading BEAUTY.

Make sure to read Luca's books too: The Wedding Debt & Marriage Debt, now available on Amazon.

You can stay up to date of new books via my website: www.clarissawild.com

I'd love to talk to you! You can find me on Facebook: www.facebook.com/ClarissaWildAuthor, make sure to click LIKE.

You can also join the Fan Club: www.facebook.com/groups/FanClubClarissaWild and talk with other readers!

Enjoyed this book? You could really help out by leaving a review on Amazon and Goodreads. Thank you!

ALSO BY CLARISSA WILD

Dark Romance

Debts & Vengeance Series
Dellucci Mafia Duet
The Debt Duet
Savage Men Series
Delirious Series
Indecent Games Series
The Company Series
FATHER

New Adult Romance

Fierce Series
Blissful Series
Ruin
Rowdy Boy & Cruel Boy

Erotic Romance

The Billionaire's Bet Series
Enflamed Series
Unprofessional Bad Boys Series

Visit Clarissa Wild's website for current titles.
www.clarissawild.com

ABOUT THE AUTHOR

Clarissa Wild is a New York Times & USA Today Bestselling author of Dark Romance and Contemporary Romance novels. She is an avid reader and writer of swoony stories about dangerous men and feisty women. Her other loves include her hilarious husband, her cutie pie son, her two crazy but cute dogs, and her ninja cat that sometimes thinks he's a dog too. In her free time, she enjoys watching all sorts of movies, playing video games, reading tons of books, and cooking her favorite meals.

Want to be informed of new releases and special offers? Sign up for Clarissa Wild's newsletter on her website www.clarissawild.com.

Visit Clarissa Wild on Amazon for current titles.

Printed in Great Britain
by Amazon